Hi, I'm JIMMY!

Like me, you probably noticed the world is run by adults.
But ask yourself: Who would do the best job
of making books that *kids* will love?
Yeah. **Kids!**

So that's how the idea of JIMMY books came to life.
We want every JIMMY book to be so good
that when you're finished, you'll say,
"PLEASE GIVE ME ANOTHER BOOK!"

Give this one a try and see if you agree.
(If not, you're probably an adult!)

JIMMY PATTERSON BOOKS FOR YOUNG READERS

James Patterson Presents

Sci-Fi Junior High by John Martin and Scott Seegert

Sci-Fi Junior High: Crash Landing by John Martin and Scott Seegert

How to Be a Supervillain by Michael Fry

How to Be a Supervillain: Born to Be Good by Michael Fry

How to Be a Supervillain: Bad Guys Finish First by Michael Fry

The Unflushables by Ron Bates

Ernestine, Catastrophe Queen by Merrill Wyatt

Scouts by Shannon Greenland

The Middle School Series by James Patterson

Middle School, The Worst Years of My Life

Middle School: Get Me Out of Here!

Middle School: Big Fat Liar

Middle School: How I Survived Bullies, Broccoli, and Snake Hill

Middle School: Ultimate Showdown

Middle School: Save Rafe!

Middle School: Just My Rotten Luck

Middle School: Dog's Best Friend

Middle School: Escape to Australia

Middle School: From Hero to Zero

Middle School: Born to Rock

The I Funny Series by James Patterson

I Funny

I Even Funnier

I Totally Funniest

I Funny TV

I Funny: School of Laughs

The Nerdiest, Wimpiest, Dorkiest I Funny Ever

The House of Robots Series by James Patterson

House of Robots

House of Robots: Robots Go Wild!

House of Robots: Robot Revolution

For exclusives, trailers, and other information, visit jimmypatterson.org.

HOW TO BE A SUPERVILLAIN

BAD GUYS FINISH FIRST

Michael Fry

JIMMY Patterson Books
LITTLE, BROWN AND COMPANY
New York Boston London

JIMMY Patterson Books / Little, Brown and Company
Hachette Book Group
1290 Avenue of the Americas, New York, NY 10104
JimmyPatterson.org

First Edition: May 2019

JIMMY Patterson Books is an imprint of Little, Brown and Company, a division of Hachette Book Group, Inc. The Little, Brown name and logo are trademarks of Hachette Book Group, Inc. The JIMMY Patterson Books® name and logo are trademarks of JBP Business, LLC.

The publisher is not responsible for websites (or their content) that are not owned by the publisher.

The Hachette Speakers Bureau provides a wide range of authors for speaking events. To find out more, go to hachettespeakersbureau.com or call (866) 376-6591.

ISBN 978-0-316-42019-8
LCCN: 2019936673

10 9 8 7 6 5 4 3 2 1

LSC-C

Printed in the United States of America

For my sister Sue.
Go, Giants!

HOW TO BE A
SUPERVILLAIN
BAD GUYS FINISH FIRST

PROLOGUE

Imagine a world a lot like yours. But different. There are people and houses and neighborhoods and cities and clueless parents and annoying brothers and sisters (just like yours!). But they're different. How different? Imagine living next door to this guy.

MOLDY DAVE

This is a super. He or she or it (don't ask) could be a superhero or a supervillain. They're not so easy to tell apart. You have to know what to look for.

And, of course, they all have some weird superpower.

But supers also mow their lawns...

VROOM

Take out the trash...

And put on their tights one leg at a time. Just like you!

That is, if you wore brightly colored tights, which you don't, because they're hot and smelly and removing them often results in accidents.

Welcome to my world. I'm Victor Spoil and I'm a junior supervillain. I'm the son and grandson and great grandson and great-great grandson of supervillains.

I've saved the world a couple times now (with my super tickling superpowers).

Seriously. It's true. You've never heard of me, but that's how it is with saving the world. All saving. No glory. Or, a little glory.

The glory fades and then you're back at school at Junior Super Academy and you're falling asleep in Super Costume Care and Maintenance Class.

I'm getting a little tired of this super world. It can get quite silly.

For example, all the battles are fake.

Except when they're not.

And no one seems to appreciate my saving-the-world skills for more than a week or so. People have short memories. They're easily distracted. I blame smartphones. And discrimination against junior supervillains with silly tickling powers.

That's why this summer I'm taking some time off to explore other career opportunities.

It has to be something interesting, with regular hours and air-conditioning (supershorts can super chafe). No superbattles. No world saving. No angry civilians with dented SUVs from nearsighted supers with poor aim.

And absolutely no alien super collectors in spaceships that run on lava like the last time I saved the world.

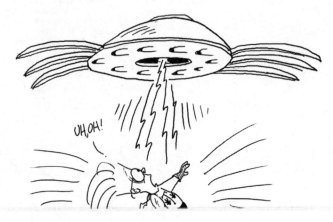

I just want something that makes sense. Something predictable. Something calm. No chaos. Order. I like order.

And there is this one other teeny-tiny thing.

Almost not worth mentioning. You remember my super tickling power. Well, lately it's been getting a little out of control. Especially when I'm stressed.

See? I clearly need a break before I hurt someone. Not that I could ever really hurt anybody. At least not intentionally.

What I needed was to spend a quiet summer at the one place least likely to be crushed by a giant swamp worm.

That's right. I'm going to Library Sleepaway Camp this summer. I'll be a junior librarian. That's like a real librarian except without the sensible shoes (you have to earn those).

WHOA!

QUITE SENSIBLE

It's going be fun and interesting and completely lacking in silly and/or life-threatening super shenanigans. Also, very orderly. Not chaos-y.

I'm so psyched.

WHAT COULD POSSIBLY GO WRONG?

CHAPTER 1

It was the last day of class before summer break at Junior Super Academy and I was saying my good-byes to my junior super friend (who happens to be a girl) Octavia Sparkle and my junior super roommate (who happens to be super weird) Javy Garcia.

It had been an eventful year. Octavia and Javy helped me save the world for the second time. Octavia's superpower is shooting out tiny annoying shiny specks that stick to everything.

NON-TOXIC

EAT GLITTER!

GLUTEN FREE

LOCALLY SOURCED

Javy reads minds.

Sort of. He has dyslexia.

"You're really doing this Library Sleepaway Camp thing?" asked Octavia. "While the rest of us are at Junior Super Summer Camp kicking butt and taking names?"

"I'm taking the name Basil. But just for the summer," said Javy.

"Yup. Can't wait," I said.

Javy put his hands on my head.

"I'm telling the truth," I said.

"Hey," said Octavia, "you be you, but...a librarian?"

I said, "I love books. I like to read. I like to know stuff. Stuff that matters."

"Wait. Being a super doesn't matter?" said Octavia.

"I like being a super," interrupted Javy, "though I'd trade mind reading for shooting lightning bolts out of my butt."

Octavia and I stared at Javy.

He explained, "Lightning-bolt-shooting eyes and fingers have been taken. But butts are wide open."

"Supers matter," I said. "Sort of. For entertainment purposes only."

"But you're a super and you saved the world," said Octavia.

"Twice," added Javy.

"I know. It's just not something I want to get in the habit of," I said.

Octavia said, "You don't want to get in the habit of helping people?"

"No. I just want to help in a different way," I said. "A safer way. A more orderly way. A less... you know...silly way?"

"Silly? Seriously?" said Octavia. "Your super-power is tickling."

"What was that?" said Octavia.

"Nothing," I said.

"That wasn't tickling," said Javy. "That was exploding."

"You haven't hurt anyone, have you?" said Octavia.

"No. Of course not. I could never hurt anyone," I protested.

"Then again, you *are* the son of supervillains," said Javy.

Wait. Is that what's going on? Am I supposed to be dangerous? Am I supposed to lose control?

"I'm worried about you, Victor," said Octavia.

"I'm worried about him, too," said a voice behind us.

It was Niles. Niles used to be the Mean Kid on Campus. We used to hate each other. Mostly because he was a jerk.

PERFECT HAIR

PERFECT BRITISH ACCENT

PERFECT SMILE

PERFECT TANGERINE AXE BODY WASH SCENT

TOTAL JERK

But then I saved his life once. That's when he decided I was okay.

Niles said, "If you blow yourself up, then I'll never get a chance to save your life and get even."

Octavia said, "Niles, this isn't about you."

Niles looked confused. "I don't understand. It's always about me."

Octavia rolled her eyes.

"Victor's going to Library Sleepaway Camp instead of super camp with us," said Javy.

"That's really, really stupid. Wait. No. My bad. Until I save your life, I can't tell you you're being a complete butt-head."

Remind me never to let Niles save my life.

We all stood there for a few long, awkward seconds, then…

Wait. What?

CHAPTER 2

Meet my supervillain parents: Rupert and Olivia Spoil, a.k.a. the Spoil Sports. Today, I'm watching them fake-battle Big Hands and Politeness Man. Big Hands is the one with the big hands.

"I'm okay," said Dad. "You know, except for this burn on my belly."

He was really hurt! Really, really hurt! *I* hurt my dad!

Mom freaked. "What's the matter with you?"

I said. "I don't know! I just…"

"You're a tickler, not an exploder!" said Dad.

"You hurt your dad and you almost took Big Hands' hands off," said Mom.

Big Hands waved. "I'm good!"

"Are you feeling okay?" asked Mom as she checked me for a fever.

Of course, I wasn't okay. It happened *again*. And this time I hurt someone. Maybe Javy was right. Maybe being a supervillain is catching up to me.

HEY! WAIT UP, TICKLE BOY!

Dad shook his head. "You've got to get your head in the game, son!"

"You're right, I said. "It really is just a game."

Mom said, "It's not a game to us." She pointed to the sparse crowd. "It's not a game to them."

"Reality is in the eye of the beholder," said a voice behind me.

I turned around. It was my old buddy the Smear.

The Smear was my first super teacher. He and I saved the world together. Twice. I know. He doesn't look like much, but with the help of his ninja mice platoon he gets the job done.

SINISTER EYEBROWS

SINISTER SMILE

COOL NINJA MICE

SINISTER PAUNCH

I pointed to Big Hands. "None of this is real."

Big Hands frowned. "I'm just as God and the bite of a radioactive squirrel made me."

"No," I said. "That's not what I meant."

"What did you mean?" asked the Smear.

I don't know what I meant. It's fine if some supers want to pretend. But I was tired of pretending to be a supervillain. And now I'm not even pretending. Now I might be on the verge of hurting someone.

But all I said was, "Nothing."

"We understand this whole super life may not be for you," said Dad. "That's why you're going to try this librarian thing. To find out for yourself."

"When does Library Sleepaway Camp start?" asked the Smear.

"Tomorrow," I said.

"So soon?" said Mom. "Are you packed?"

"Ick," said Mom. "Couldn't you be a bit messier?"

"Ironed underwear is never a good look for a supervillain," said Dad.

I smiled, "But it's a great look for a librarian."

"Let's get the car," said Dad.

Mom and Dad left as the Smear and I looked on.

The Smear said, "It's hard for supervillain parents to show it, but they really do love you."

"I know, they just don't understand that I need to figure this out for myself."

"They're letting you do this. And you *will* figure it out. But promise me you'll be careful."

"It's a library!"

"And the Boston Common, where you saved the world the first time, was just a park. And Monument Valley, where you saved it a second time, was just a pile of rocks."

"Do you know something I don't know?" I asked.

"I know lots of things you don't know. For instance, I know how to do this..."

I frowned. "You know what I mean. Is there some sort of danger? Are the librarians some sort of zombies that feed off well-read brains?"

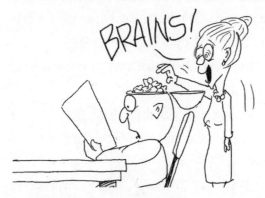

The Smear said, "No. They're vampires. They'll suck the super right out of you."

I smiled. "You don't want me to do this."

"Victor, your parents and I, we just want you to be happy. Safe and happy. But just remember, who you are has a way of catching up to you."

Who I am? Does he mean, a supervillain?

Before I could ask, the Smear was walking away.

"I'm rooting for you, Victor," said the Smear. "No matter where you are or what's going on, you always do the right thing."

And he was gone.

CHAPTER 3

Mom and Dad dropped me off at Library Sleep-away Camp.

He never saw the butt laser coming.

Dad stared. "It's awfully quiet in there."

"It's supposed to be quiet," I said. "It's a library."

"Too quiet," said Mom, looking worried.

I shook my head. "What do you think is going to happen? Death by paper cut?"

"Death by boredom," said Dad.

I sighed. "I'm doing this. It's what I want."

"Like you wanted to be a pharmacist," said Mom.

I glared at them. "I was four. It was a phase. This is serious."

"He was so cute in his white lab coat, counting pills," said Dad.

OKAY... IT'S TWO SWEET TARTS TWICE A DAY WITH JELL-O. AND ABSOLUTELY NO OPERATING HEAVY MACHINERY.

"Always so particular about everything," said Mom.

Dad said, "Everything in its place. Everything just so. Victor always has to have *order*."

Mom frowned, "Never chaos."

"You should try it sometime," said Dad. "Chaos is fun!"

"Enough!" I snapped.

Mom smiled. "There's our little supervillain."

"He's in there," said Dad. "Hiding."

"I'm going," I said.

I headed for the front door of the library.

"You forgot something!" yelled Mom.

I stopped. "What?"

I turned and looked back. It's true. They did love me. And I loved them.

It's just that at that particular moment I didn't *like* them very much.

CHAPTER 4

I opened the door to the library. And it hit me.

WHOOSH!

The smell.

You probably think I think books smell like sunshine. Or puppies. Or rainbows. Or unicorns (that poop rainbows).

It's true! →

No. Books smell like mystery. Books smell like an old donut in the back of the refrigerator. It might be good. It might not. What's inside? Is it fun? Is it scary? Is it boring? Will it kill me? Will it save me? Will it take me where I never knew I wanted to go?

WHEEE!

SPRINKLES

"I think they smell like pudding," said a woman's voice.

"I think they smell like warm socks right out of the dryer," said another woman.

"I think they smell like the last leaf of autumn," said a third woman. "The one that falls to your feet and crumbles into a thousand pieces of possibility."

I turned to see three women.

"You must be Victor," said the woman in the center. "I'm the head librarian, Mrs. Wibble."

Mrs. Wibble looked like a librarian. Sweet, patient, with just a glint of steel in her eye. Or was that library paste?

"Hello," I said.

Mrs. Wibble gestured to the other women. "This is Ms. Orion and this is Mrs. Rotel."

"Charmed to make your acquaintance," said Ms. Orion.

"He doesn't look like a supervillain," said Mrs. Rotel.

"I'm not!" I said a little too loud.

"No," said Mrs. Wibble. "No, today you're a junior librarian."

"With a lot to learn," said Ms. Orion.

I looked around. The library was huge. Sunlight streamed through floor-to-ceiling windows illuminating endless rows of books. Tiny dust motes danced in the sunbeams as though they were excited to be there. Because, apparently, no one else was.

"Where is everyone?" I asked.

There was a pause as the three librarians shared a look.

"Slow day," said Mrs. Wibble.

"Mondays are always slow," said Ms. Orion.

Mrs. Rotel added, "And Tuesdays. And Wednesdays. And..."

Mrs. Wibble snapped, "Enough."

Mrs. Rotel mimed zipping her lips shut.

"Not everyone likes to read," I said.

"We've noticed," said Mrs. Wibble.

"And we're working on it," said Ms. Orion, with a tone that suggested it was not only true, but certain.

There was a beat of silence. Then...

"Would you like to help us shelve some books?" said Mrs. Wibble.

"Would I!" I piped.

I know. I shouldn't pipe. It's unbecoming. But I don't care. I like books. I like reading them. I like holding them. I like shelving them. In their

proper place, according to the Dewey Decimal
System.

MELVILLE DEWEY

INVENTED LIBRARY CLASSIFICATION SYSTEM →

100 PHILOSOPHY
200 RELIGION
300 SOCIAL SCIENCES
400 LANGUAGE
500 SCIENCE
600 TECH

WAS KNOWN FOR HIS YODELING SKILLS*

* I MADE THAT PART UP.

Mrs. Wibble handed me a book. "Go for it."
It was a book on owls.

OWLS I HAVE KNOWN

MORTIMER WINKLEFLOSS

Mortimer had known a lot of owls.

"Okay," I said out loud, "This is a work of non-fiction. And it's about animals. So that means it should be in the 500s, for science. Then the 590s, for animals. Then 598 for birds."

"Wow," said Ms. Orion. "He didn't even have to look at the spine."

"I spend a lot of time in libraries," I said.

"Obviously," said Mrs. Wibble.

I headed toward the proper stack. The bird books were on the top shelf. I rolled a ladder over and started to climb. I stopped halfway up. There was another book that caught my eye. It was mis-shelved; it didn't belong in the science section. I pulled it out.

I smiled. No need for that now.

What the…

"Uh-oh," said Mrs. Wibble.

CHAPTER 5

Wait. I'm in a library. This shouldn't be happening
in a library.

CRASH!

Yet it is happening.
Wait. What exactly *is* happening?

What did I say before? Something about a nice quiet summer shelving books? Something about air-conditioning. Something about *no super stuff*!

I'm not sure, but destroying books on your first day as a junior librarian is probably not the best look.

Poor Mr. Winklefloss.

"Victor, it's okay," said Mrs. Wibble. "You didn't mean to do it."

CHAPTER 6

"It was an accident," said Mrs. Wibble.

"No," I replied. "I don't think it was. Something's wrong with me. My superpower is supposed to be *tickling!*"

"Just a glitch," said Mrs. Rotel.

"A bug," agreed Ms. Orion.

Mrs. Wibble said, "Soon, it will all be better."

"Soon? What are you talking about?" I said as I looked around. "And what's going on here? Who were those ninjas? And..."

I stared at Mrs. Wibble. "This isn't really a library, is it?"

Mrs. Wibble smiled. "It's *more* than a library."

I said, "More?"

"*Way* more," said Ms. Orion and Mrs. Rotel at the same time.

Mrs. Wibble motioned to the check-out desk. "Follow me, Victor."

I followed. We all went behind the check-out desk. Mrs. Wibble pulled out a gold library card.

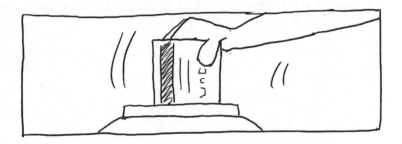

KA-CHUNK

WHIRRR...

WHIRRR

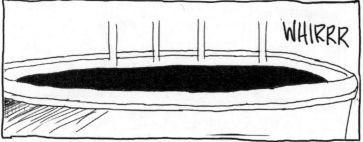

WHIRRR

The front desk continued downward for what seemed like several stories. Recessed lighting turned on and music played as we descended.

We stopped. There was a long, dramatic pause, then two large elevator doors opened, revealing a massive underground control room.

I turned to Mrs. Wibble. "We won't be shelving any more books, will we?"

She shook her head. "Not today."

CHAPTER 7

We walked to a conference room off the main floor. Inside was a digital projector and a laptop.

"We put this presentation together especially for you," said Mrs. Wibble.

"Mrs. Rotel is a whiz at PowerPoint," said Ms. Orion.

Mrs. Rotel blushed. "I've got skills."

Mrs. Wibble started the projector and picked up the clicker. "In the beginning, there was a library, and it was good."

WE LOANED BOOKS AND INTRODUCED MILLIONS TO READING. IT WAS GREAT, BUT WE WANTED MORE.

HERE YOU GO.

WE HAD THE KNOWLEDGE. WE WANTED TO USE THAT KNOWLEDGE TO HELP THE WORLD.

SO WE FOUNDED THE LEGION OF LIBRARIANS TO BRING OUR SPECIALIZED EXPERTISE IN ORGANIZATION AND SENSIBLE SHOES TO THE WORLD.

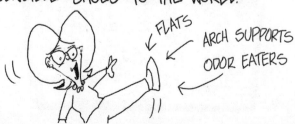

FLATS

ARCH SUPPORTS

ODOR EATERS

WE BUILT THIS UNDERGROUND DATA CENTER AND LAUNCHED A DOZEN SATELLITES WITH THE GOAL OF OBSERVING EVERY PERSON ON THE PLANET.

WITH THE HELP OF A TRILLION TERABYTES OF SOLID STATE STORAGE AND OUR PROPRIETARY ALGORITHM, WE CAN TRACK AND ANTICIPATE ALMOST EVERY HUMAN ACTION.

WITH THIS PREDICTIVE TECHNOLOGY, WE CAN INTERVENE AND PROTECT HUMANITY FROM MAKING POOR DECISIONS.

"You want to save the world," I said, "from it-self?"

"Yes," said Mrs. Wibble.

Having had some experience in world-saving, I said, "What if the world doesn't want to be saved?"

"The world doesn't know what it wants," said Ms. Orion.

"But you do?" I said.

"We're librarians," said Mrs. Rotel. "We know *everything*."

"But…"

CHAPTER 8

When most kids are shushed by librarians, they stay shushed. Not me. I'm shush-proof.

"What about free will?" I said.

"You ask a lot of questions," said Ms. Orion.

"How else is he going to learn?" asked Mrs. Wibble. "Free will isn't free, Victor."

"The cost of free will can be very high," said Ms. Orion.

"Too high," added Mrs. Rotel.

"I don't understand," I said.

"Let us demonstrate," said Mrs. Wibble. "Watch the monitor."

Mrs. Wibble spoke into an intercom, "Lucy, can you cue up Datastream 99-GS-88 for me?"

"You bet," replied Lucy.

An image of a familiar car driving through a familiar neighborhood came up on the screen.

"Hey, that's my parents' car," I said.
"Now the satellite," said Mrs. Wibble.
"What satellite?" I asked.

"Yes, it is," said Mrs. Wibble. "Show us the impact trajectory, Lucy."

I cried, "It's going to hit my parents!"

"Yes," said Ms. Orion. "And no."

"Do something!" I pleaded.

"Watch," said Mrs. Wibble.

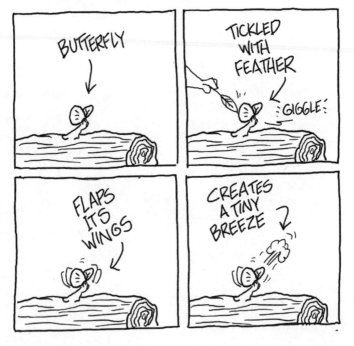

"It missed!" I cheered.

"It did," said Mrs. Wibble.

"You did that?" I asked.

Mrs. Wibble nodded. "We did."

CHAPTER 9

Okay. Let's take a second and think about this.

On the one hand, these hotshot, kick-butt, super-secret librarian wannabe world-saving warriors are completely nuts. You can't make the entire world safe for everyone. I mean, if the whole planet were completely stress-free, then, you know, no one would ever need a super to straighten things out.

ANYONE
NEED
SAVING?

NO.
WE'RE
GOOD.

No. One. Would. Ever. Need. A. Super. *Again!*

I turned to Mrs. Wibble, "If you have this power to control things, why do bad things still happen? People are still dying. Planes fall out of the sky. Volcanoes still erupt. Goat cheese still tastes like sweatsocks."

"We can't do anything about goat cheese," said Mrs. Wibble.

I pointed to the screen. "That satellite missed my parents, but it did quite a number on that Mini Cooper."

"We can't control everything," said Mrs. Wibble. "At least not yet."

"What do you mean not yet?" I said.

Mrs. Wibble pointed her clicker at the screen. "Not until we get this."

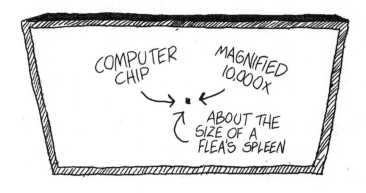

"It's an experimental computer chip," said Ms. Orion. "It's so fast it can track and predict the behavior of all seven billion people on the planet."

Mrs. Rotel added, "And render their lives happy and safe forever and ever."

I was skeptical. "That's not a thing."

Mrs. Wibble nodded. "It's a thing."

"And you have it?" I asked.

"No. But we know where it is," said Ms. Orion, as she pointed to the screen.

"That's Madge's place," I realized. "I know her."

Madge builds stuff. Like robots. She built Captain Chaos. Captain Chaos has amazing powers and can do pretty much anything. But not on his own. He's controlled by a person inside him.

He helped me the second time I saved the world. We saved it from the Commodore's evil plan to snatch all the cool supers and make them fight to the death for galactic entertainment purposes. It's a long story. You should read it.

"We know you know Madge. That's why you're going to get it for us," said Mrs. Wibble.

I said, "Wait. I am?"

CHAPTER 10

"Why don't you just get it yourself?" I asked.

Mrs. Wibble said, "We could, but you can do it faster and cleaner."

"I can?" I asked.

"Madge knows you," said Mrs. Wibble. "She won't suspect anything. You're in. You're out. And back here with the chip."

I shook my head. "Nope. No way. I'm taking a break from the whole super thing."

"Wait. Why?" said Mrs. Wibble.

"Yes," I said. "I've saved the world twice. I deserve some time off. I just want to shelve some books and help people spell stuff."

"That's a tricky one," said Ms. Orion. "*I* before *e* except when there's a *v* and no *i*."

Mrs. Wibble said, "You know you want to help us."

I did. But I didn't. I liked what they're going for. As I've told you, I prefer order to chaos. Chaos is very messy and it smells like burnt hair.

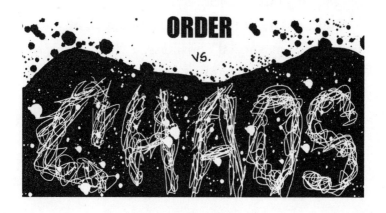

The idea of making the world a safe space for everyone is tempting. Even if it means taking away a bit of everyone's freedom. I mean who wants to be free to die from a falling satellite? Or an earthquake. Or a tornado. Or a hurricane. Or an exploding pudding factory.

See? It's just embarrassing.

But...if I help them, I'm stepping right back into the "I'm special" business. I don't want to be special. I don't want to save the world. I don't want the responsibility. Besides, I've got no control over my powers. People could get hurt.

People *have* gotten hurt.

"I pass," I said.

Mrs. Wibble said, "We can make it worth your

while. You do this one thing for us," said Mrs. Wibble. "And we'll do something for you."

I gave her a skeptical look. "Like what?"

Mrs. Rotel said, "When we have the Quantum Flux 9000, you can retire forever."

Mrs. Wibble said, "No more saving the world. Because the world won't need saving. After we have the chip, we can use it to nullify your powers. No more super tickling. No more super stuff. No more losing control and hurting people."

"You know about that?" I asked.

Mrs. Wibble smiled, "We know everything about you."

Mrs. Rotel nodded her head a bit too enthusiastically.

"All we're asking is for one last super favor,"
said Ms. Orion. "One last task. One last quest.
One last battle."

CHAPTER 11

"Okay," I said.

"Okay?" said Mrs. Wibble, like she didn't hear me right.

I said, "Yeah. I'll do it. I'll get you the chip. Then you save the world. Then you make me ordinary. You make me *safe*."

"But, you know, not too ordinary," I added. "I'd like to keep the cape and the gloves and the memories."

"We can't take away your memories," said Mrs. Wibble.

I said, "I still have some questions. Why—"

WHOOP! WHOOP! WHOOP!
INTRUDER ALERT!!

"What is that?" I cried.
"The ninja robots are back!"

CHAPTER 12

The ninja robots gained access to the elevator and reached the underground control center.

Mrs. Wibble grabbed me. "They're looking for you. We have to get you out of here!"

"Why are they after me? Who are they?"

"Not everyone wants to save the world," said Mrs. Wibble as we ran.

"You're quite special!" yelled Ms. Orion.

Mrs. Rotel cried, "Prepare the escape pod!"

The three librarians hustled me out of the conference room and through the command center.

THIS WAY!

We arrived at the opposite end of the command center. Mrs. Wibble slapped a control panel on the wall. The wall gave way, revealing...

"Get inside!" cried Mrs. Wibble.

As I jumped in the pod, I looked back across the control room.

Wait. The Smear *and* Captain Chaos were the ones attacking? With the ninja robots? It didn't make sense!

And Captain Chaos is operating by himself? That can't happen. He's a robot!

Wait. Do they know about the librarians? Or do they want chaos? What did the Smear say again?

HE SAID, "WHO YOU ARE HAS A WAY OF CATCHING UP WITH YOU."

THANKS.

Before I could make sense of it all, a panel opened in the ceiling of the command center, revealing the sky above.

Mrs. Wibble yelled, "Good luck, Victor! Get the chip and return here as fast as you can."

I watched the Smear and Captain Chaos fight the librarians. What just happened? How is Captain Chaos operating? Is he...

... ALIVE?

WHOOSH!

The escape pod cleared the library and launched a parachute. As the pod slowly drifted to the ground I could see the scale of the battle below.

This was big. Bigger than I could handle. I was going to need help.

CHAPTER 13

"What are you talking about?" said Octavia.

It was the next day. Octavia, Javy, Niles, and I were meeting at a Starbucks near the Junior Super Academy. Everyone knows when you're looking to make a super plan to save the world, the first place you go is the last place anyone would look. I learned that in Stealthy Super Planning class.

... STARBUCKS, STOP-N-SNARF, DRY CLEANERS, AND ANY BOUNCY HOUSE.

EGGPLANT*

* INSTEAD OF APPLE

I said, "Captain Chaos and the Smear were attacking me!"

"What? Why?" asked Octavia.

I said, "I don't know! But Captain Chaos was operating by himself. Like he was *alive*!"

"Slow down, cowboy," said Octavia. "Captain Chaos is a robot. Robots aren't alive."

"I'm just telling you what I saw," I said. "The Smear was *not* inside him. In fact, the Smear was leading the assault. Against me!"

"He is alive!" said Javy. "I knew it. He always had that look in his eye."

"What look is that?" said Niles.

"The 'I'm alive' look," said Javy. "It's kind of a side-eye, I'm-watching-you-because-your-fly-is-down-no-it-isn't-made-you-look look. Something like this…"

SIDE EYE

"Why are you so weird?" I asked.

IT COMES WITH THE TERRITORY!

"Moving on," I said. "I need your help to get to Madge. She built him, so if anyone can stop Captain Chaos, she can!"

Octavia raised her hand.

"You don't have to raise your hand," I said.

Octavia said, "This doesn't make any sense. The Smear and Captain Chaos are good guys! We all just saved the world together!"

"I know," I said. "But I saw what I saw."

"But there has to be some reason," said Niles. "What did the Smear say to you when you last met?"

"He said who I am has a way of catching up to me," I said.

Nobody said anything.

"It's your powers," said Octavia.

I said, "What about my...?"

"You're losing control of them," said Javy. "Remember that explosion the other day. That was no tickle."

"Wait," I said. "You think they're trying to stop me because they think I'm turning into a real *supervillain*?!"

Octavia said, "I'm sure they just want to protect you."

Or stop me. Or stop the Legion of Librarians from making the world a safer place.

But I didn't tell my friends that. They might not help me if they knew the whole story about the librarians controlling everyone to keep them safe. That by helping the librarians my powers will be gone and I won't be a danger to anyone. If they knew all that, they might try to stop me.

And I can't let that happen.

"Will you help me?" I asked.

"Wait," said Niles. "Isn't this a job for the Authority? They're in charge of all the superheroes and supervillains. Why do *we* always have to save the world?"

Good question. Think fast.

"I put a call in to Norman," I lied. Norman used to work for the Authority but then he became the president of the Junior Super Academy. Still, I didn't know anyone else in the Authority. They didn't seem to do much. "But he's on vacation."

There was a beat. I expected three eye rolls, but nothing.

"Norman's useless," said Octavia.

That's true.

"*Of course* we'll help you," said Octavia. "We trust you."

"You're our friend," said Javy.

"I might get a chance to save you this time," said Niles.

I hope not.

Javy grinned, "This is just like *Mission Impossible!*"

Octavia said, "You mean like how the plot is so complicated it's really hard to follow?"

"Exactly!" cried Javy.

I sighed. "It's not that complicated."

"Isn't Tom Cruise like a hundred and thirty years old now?" asked Niles.

Octavia smiled. "That's ridiculous. He doesn't look a day over ninety."

Javy said, "He does all his own stunts."

The good news? The gang's back together.
The bad news? The gang's back together.

CHAPTER 14

First, we needed to buy enough time for Octavia, Niles, and Javy to go to Madge's trailer with me. They told their parents they were joining me for Library Sleepaway Camp.

This was tricky for Javy since his parents are invisible.

Then we had to arrange transportation to Madge's lab. Super-Uber didn't go there so we had to take Bee Boy's blimp.

BEE BOY'S BLIMP →

Blimps aren't the fastest way to travel. We had plenty of time to sit and wait and avoid eye contact.

Octavia kept staring at me. She looked concerned. She *should* be concerned. It's not like I was 100 percent positive I was doing the right thing. But what about my powers? I can't control them. Look what I did to my dad. The librarians can stop that. All they want is to save the world. And bring order. I like order. Who doesn't like order? Order's good? Right?

"What's wrong?" asked Octavia.

"I'm worried about you," said Octavia.

"I'm fine," I said. "I'm just trying to do the right thing."

"I know. You always do. Eventually."

Yeah. Eventually. Was she onto me? Did she know there was more to my story? It was like she had some super-glitter-mind-truth thing and she could see into my soul.

Octavia smiled. "It's all going to be okay. I trust you. Niles and Javy trust you. You wouldn't steer us wrong."

"...there's something I have to tell you."
"It's okay. I understand," she said.
"No, you don't understand," I said.

"What the—"
Javy and Niles ran over from the cockpit.

CHAPTER 15

There's a whole list of things you don't want to hear when you're in a blimp. "We're going down," is number three.

1. IT'S JUST A SMALL LEAK.
2. FIRE UP THE GRILL!
3. WE'RE GOING DOWN!
4. WHO FARTED?
5. HAS ANYONE SEEN MY VELOCIRAPTOR?

"We're being attacked!" yelled Niles.

I looked out the window. What I saw can only be described as odd.

Javy asked, "Are those...?"

"Flying laser hamsters!" I yelled. "They're attacking the ship!"

Now there's a sentence you've never read before. You're welcome.

I looked down. We were headed straight for a jagged mountaintop.

We were only about halfway to Madge's place. If we crashed, we'd never get there. That is, if we even survived the crash. We were headed down fast.

"Brace yourselves!" I cried.

We waited for impact. And waited. And waited. But nothing happened. I turned and peeked out the window. The mountaintop was gone, replaced by a lush meadow.

We landed. No crash. No broken limbs. Just a soft thud as we settled to rest.

"Where are we?" asked Octavia.

I said, "I have no idea."

"Try Google Maps," said Niles.

Javy checked his phone. "No bars. There are never any bars. Why can't we have a super adventure somewhere with decent cell reception?"

Niles looked out the window. "What do the flying laser hamsters want?"

"To eat our spleens," said Javy, confidently.

"They're not going to eat our spleens," I said, less confidently.

"Why don't we just ask them what they want?" said Octavia.

"Victor? Is that you?" came a familiar voice from outside.

We opened the blimp door to the sight of an old friend.

IT'S MOLDY DAVE!

HIDY, HO!

CHAPTER 16

"Moldy Dave, what are you doing here?" I asked.

"This is my secret lair," replied Moldy Dave. "You set off my flying-laser-hamster security system."

"I thought we were about to crash into the top of a mountain," said Octavia.

Moldy Dave nodded. "Holographic camouflage. You know, to keep out the tourists."

"Tourists? We're in the middle of nowhere," said Niles.

"After I helped you save the world the last time, I got sort of famous," said Moldy Dave.

This was true. Moldy Dave played a pivotal role in our take down of the Commodore. He really threw himself into the fight.

Moldy Dave said, "Being recognized was nice at first. I made a lot of money. They put my face on everything."

"But then came the dark side of fame. The wild parties. The rabid fans. The root beer float addiction. I couldn't go anywhere without the paparazzi all over the place," said Moldy Dave.

He continued, "I just wanted some privacy. So, I came here. Just me and my flying laser hamster security force."

"So, what brings you guys here?" asked Dave. I quickly got him up to speed.

"Wow!" said Dave. "How can I help?"

"I don't think there's anything you can do," I said. "We're miles from Madge's hideout with no way of getting there now that our blimp is down."

"Yeah, sorry about that," said Dave. "But I think I can get you there."

Moldy Dave pulled out a key fob and punched a button.

≡ BEEP! ≡

Slowly at first, then more quickly, an invisible monster minivan began to appear.

"We're saved!" I cried. "Thank you, Moldy Dave!"

"Yeah, what a stroke of luck," said Octavia.

"What?" I said.

"We're flying in a blimp on our way to Madge's when all of sudden we're shot out of the sky and land on Moldy Dave's front porch. Then he just happens to have a monster minivan to take us the rest of the way?"

She had a point. She always has a point. But we didn't have time to ask questions. I needed to get the Quantum Flux 9000 chip to the Legion of Librarians and save the world from Captain Chaos and the Smear and falling satellites.

Onward.

CHAPTER 17

We made fast work of the miles between us and Madge's place.

OVER MOUNTAINS

UNDER SEAS

THROUGH RAIN, SLEET, SNOW AND FROGS ALL AT THE SAME TIME.

We arrived at the foot of Madge's hideout and

hid in the surrounding forest to discuss our elaborate, thoroughly-thought-out, foolproof plan.

Fortunately, Octavia had an idea...

"Remember the last time we asked for help?"
I said. "She sent her robot vampires, mummies,
and zombies after us."

"She'll help us," said Octavia, "when she sees
we have her precious robot chihuahua!"

We knew from our last super adventure that Madge was uncomfortably close to her robot chihuahua, Larry.

I dunno. The plan seemed kind of dumb. But it's not like I had a better idea.

"Okay. Let's do it," I said.

Javy raised his hand.

I said, "Javy, you really don't have to raise your hand."

Javy said, "I'd just like to say, for the record, that I'm super excited to be super-adventuring again with all of you."

"That's nice," I said. "But…"

Javy continued, "And we're surrounded by bears."

CHAPTER 18

Bears. Of *course* we're surrounded by bears. Why wouldn't we be surrounded by bears? It's not like my stealing this chip wasn't going to be hard enough. Now I have to deal with hungry bears.

I THINK THEY'RE DROOLING

NOT A GOOD SIGN.

"Maybe they're not hungry," said Javy.
"What else would they be?" I asked.

Javy said, "Sad."

"Huh?" I said.

"I read their minds. They're bummed. They used to have jobs, but then they got fired. And now they're depressed."

"A job? Wait. They're bears!"

But Javy had already sprung into action.

Javy turned and explained, "They're bear-moat bears. They used to work for the Commodore in his bear moat, then the Smear hired them, but now they work for someone else."

"Wait. Hold on," I said. "These are bear-moat bears. They're dangerous. They really will eat us!"

Javy put his hands on one bear's head. "Whoa.

No. Nobody's going to get eaten. These are vegan bears."

"They're *my* bears!" shouted a familiar voice.

We turned around to see Madge step into the light.

"You destroyed all my robot paranormals, so I had to improvise. Unfortunately, bear-moat bears aren't very threatening."

NOT TOO THREATENING

"We need your help," I said.

"I know," said Madge. "But..."

THE CHIP ISN'T HERE.

"What chip?" asked Octavia.

"Yeah, what chip?" asked Niles.

"Sour cream and onion?" asked Javy. "I love sour cream and onion chips!"

UH, OH.

CHAPTER 19

"The chip the librarians want isn't here," said Madge. "It was never here."

"Victor, what chip?" asked Octavia. "I knew there was something you weren't telling us."

I had no choice. I had to tell them everything.

QUANTUM FLUX 9000 CONTROL THE WORLD SAVED MY PARENTS TAKE AWAY MY POWERS.

There was silence. A long silence. Too long.

"You lied to us," said Octavia.

"Not really," I said. "I just didn't tell you everything."

"Why?" asked Javy. "Don't you trust us?"

I said, "Of course! But...I don't know. I was worried you'd try to stop me."

"Gee," said Octavia. "Insane librarians want to control the world. Nothing weird about that."

"My powers," I said. "They said they'd take away my powers."

"You *want* to lose your powers?" said Javy.

"I *have* to lose my powers," I said.

"Why?" asked Niles.

"Because I could hurt someone again!" I screamed.

"You could never hurt anybody," said Octavia.

That did it. No one ever listens to me. I could feel my powers surging.

CHAPTER 20

"I don't have it," said Madge.

WHERE IS IT?!

"I might know how to get it?" said Madge.

"Show me! Now!" I yelled.

Okay. Sure, I was a little panicked. But I have almost no control over my powers anymore. I really don't want to hurt anyone again. I promise,

when this is all over, to go back and apologize for
being such a super jerk.

Yeah, that's going to be fun.

"This way," said Madge.

I started to follow Madge out of the clearing.
But then I turned back to make sure everyone
was okay.

Good. I haven't hurt anyone. I mean…I haven't hurt anyone permanently. Yet.

Madge approached what looked like a large tree. She pulled on a branch and a sliding door in the trunk opened.

Inside the trunk was a spiral stairway leading down.

I said, "I thought the double-wide at the top of your hill was your lair."

Madge started down the stairs. "That's just the tip of the iceberg, kid. I do all my important work underground."

I followed her down the stairs. And down and down and…you get the idea.

We finally reached a door that opened into a dark corridor.

"Where are we going?" I asked.

"You'll see."

Actually, I couldn't see anything.

Then suddenly all the lights came on and I still couldn't see anything.

Then I heard a...

...behind me. And a...

...in front of me.

My eyes slowly adjusted. I was trapped.

Through the bars on the window I could see Madge. She was on a phone.

"Yes, he's fine," said Madge. "I'll bring him to you soon."

I started pounding on the door. *"Bring me where?"*

CHAPTER 21

I had a dream.

I was back at school. Octavia, Javy, and Niles were there. We were at lunch in the Junior Super Academy Cafetorium. It was Taco and Tots Tuesday. Except in the dream, the tacos were huge and filled with squid.

I don't know why they were filled with squid. It's a dream. Squid happens. Let's move on.

So, we were eating (the tots, not the squid) and someone made a joke and we all laughed and then Javy turned into a toad.

Which was weird, but not for a dream. No, the weird part came next. Javy opened his mouth and out popped a small fly.

It was just a little thing. Harmless. Or so I thought.

Suddenly, the little fly hopped onto my nose and whispered...

Well, that was mean. Mostly true, but mean (especially the bat poop part). I was handling it fine until this nasty fly went over the line...

And I lost it.

Big time.

CHAPTER 22

BANG! BANG! BANG!

I opened my eyes. I was lying down. I tried to
move, but I couldn't. My arms and legs were tied
down.

BANG! BANG! BANG!

I looked toward the noise. On the other side of the room, Madge was holding an acetylene torch, the kind you use to weld stuff. She was banging it on something hidden from my view.

Madge looked up and said to someone out of sight, "I don't know what's wrong with him."

Then I hear a familiar voice, "Wake up, you old bucket of bolts!"

It's the Smear! And he's here!

Okay, I'll stop now. But it was the Smear. I'd know his voice anywhere.

HE WAS FINE WHEN I BROUGHT HIM IN.

Who was fine?

That's when I heard another familiar voice.

It was Captain Chaos! And he was talking!

CHAPTER 23

The Smear turned to look at me. "You're awake."

"Where am I?" I asked.

"You're safe," said the Smear.

"You can't hurt yourself here. Or anyone else."
said the Smear.

I said, "You don't know that."

Madge said, "Those are titanium restraints. Even Captain Chaos can't break those."

"Hello, Victor," said Captain Chaos.

"You're alive," I said. "How is that possible?"

Madge and the Smear and Captain Chaos all traded a look.

"Should we tell him?" asked Captain Chaos.

"We have to tell him," said the Smear.

"This is a bad idea," said Madge.

The Smear eyed Madge. "Tell him."

"No, you."

"Rock paper scissors?" offered the Smear.

"Just tell him!" shouted Madge.

THE QUANTUM 9000 IS INSIDE CAPTAIN CHAOS.

"How did you know?" whispered the Smear.

"It makes sense," I said. "The thing I need to save the world from myself is inside the thing I made up to save the world...and myself."

"You're on the wrong side here, Victor," said the Smear. "The Legion of Librarians are not your friends. They're nobody's friends. They just want order and control no matter what the cost."

"They saved my parents," I pointed out. "They want to save the world. And save others from me."

"They want to take away free will," said Captain Chaos. "That's not living. That's just existing."

"That's funny coming from a robot," I said.

"Yes," said Captain Chaos. "I'm a robot. A robot, who, thanks to Madge's chip, is alive. I have free will. I get to decide. And I decide I want to be free to live my life how I want, no matter the risks."

"Victor, do you understand what will happen if the librarians get the chip?" asked Madge.

"The world will be safe," I said. "Safe for everyone and safe from me."

"You're never going to hurt anyone," said the Smear.

"How do you know? Are you going to keep me locked up forever?" I asked.

"We'll figure something out," said the Smear.

No. They weren't going to figure anything out. Because there wasn't anything to figure out. I'm a danger to myself and others. If I don't get the chip the world is at risk. Forever.

"Victor, what are you doing?" said the Smear.

BOOM

CHAPTER 24

"Victor, calm down," said the Smear.

"I am calm. I've never been calmer in my life. I know exactly what I need to do."

GIVE. ME. THE. CHIP.

"No," said the Smear. "We will fight you. We don't want to, but we will fight you. We will *all* fight you."

That's when the back wall opened and revealed everyone.

Octavia, Javy, Niles, Moldy Dave, all the lame supers. Even Anvil Head.

Me vs. everyone. Sounds familiar.

Octavia came up to me. She put her hands on my chest.

STOP! JUST STOP!

"I don't have a choice," I said.

"That's the whole point," said Octavia. "Now you have a choice. If you get this chip and give it to the librarians, you won't have a choice. None of us will."

"I don't have a choice," I repeated as I walked up to Captain Chaos. "Hand it over."

The Smear got between us.

Captain Chaos turned toward the others. "Victor's right. He doesn't have a choice.

THAT'S WHY I'M GIVING HIM THE CHIP.

"No!" cried the Smear.

Captain Chaos stood next to me to face the others. "Yes. Madge, take out the chip and hand it to Victor."

"Why?" said the Smear.

"We can't fight for free choice by taking it away," said Captain Chaos.

"Yes, we can!" said Madge. "Victor's just one kid, think of the whole world."

Captain Chaos looked at me. "Victor's more than one kid. Victor is special. He deserves to choose for himself. I trust him. He'll make the right choice."

"Well, I don't trust him," said the Smear, taking a fighting stance.

"This is a mistake," said the Smear.

Captain Chaos looked at me and smiled. "We shall see. Madge?"

Madge walked over. She opened Captain Chaos's back. I looked deep into his eyes.

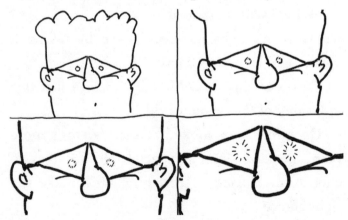

Madge handed me the chip. I looked at it. Then looked at everyone.

"Victor..." said Octavia.

CHAPTER 25

Well, that was…sad.

But necessary.

Not a lot of good options.

BAD OPTIONS

1.) GIVE BACK THE CHIP, I HURT SOMEONE
2.) BURY THE CHIP, I HURT SOMEONE.
3.) DESTROY THE CHIP, I HURT SOMEONE.
4.) GIVE THE CHIP TO THE LIBRARIANS.
   MAYBE I DON'T HURT ANYONE.

I exited Madge's secret lair. You might think it was difficult finding my way out, but not really.

I came out through Madge's double-wide trailer on the surface. Now what? How was I going to get the chip back to the librarians? It was a long way back to The Near-Sighted Boy Memorial Library.

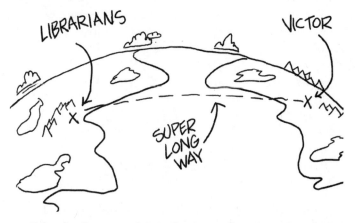

I looked around Madge's trailer. Maybe there was a spare space plane or a transporter or even a blimp.

No such luck.

I was about to think this was all a stupid idea and I should give Captain Chaos back his chip, when I saw something interesting around back.

It looked like a jet pack. Sort of.

Sure. Why not? I've seen stranger stuff. I saw stranger stuff ten minutes ago!

I strapped it on, gritted my teeth, and flipped the switch.

Nothing. I checked to see if it had gas.

Ah, it was a solar jet pack. Very environmentally conscious of Madge. I'd have to congratulate her after this whole save-the-world-from-myself thing is over.

I turned the solar panels toward the sun and flipped the switch.

Isn't technology wonderful?

Check that.

CHAPTER 26

I zipped along for a few hours. Other than a few stowaways it wasn't too bad.

The only problem with a solar jet pack is that it's a solar jet pack.

I was making good progress, but it was going to take forever to get back to the Legion of Librarians. I needed a faster way.

That's when I thought, *Hey, go to a library.* They've got to all be interconnected. There's probably some underground hyperloop that connects them. Or they can call for the Legion of Librarians' space plane to come get me. Or they can plug in the chip remotely. Makes sense that the librarians would have the whole planet wired.

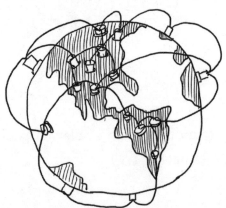

I instantly rerouted to the nearest library.

I stashed the jet pack and entered.

"Smells like pudding, right?" said the librarian behind the desk.

"Yeah, pudding," I said. "Listen, can you help me get in touch with the Legion of Librarians?"

"The what?"

"The Legion of Librarians. I'm helping them save the world. I have the chip."

"Original or cool ranch?"

"Excuse me?"

"Salt and vinegar or BBQ?" asked the librarian.

"Computer," I said. "The Quantum Flux 9000. You librarians are going to be using it to control everyone and everything so you can make the world perfectly safe."

"Why would we want to do that?"

I said, "To make things safe. Also, you're going to take away my powers so I don't hurt anybody."

"Your powers?"

"My superpowers. I have super tickling powers. I hurt people. It's a long story."

UM...
SUPER
TICKLING?
RIGHT.

The librarian frowned. "Should I be calling the police?"

"No! You should be calling the Legion of Librarians! I have the chip! Together we can save the world!"

"To make it safe?"

"Yes! I said that!"

"Okay, let me get this straight. You have a computer chip that can control everyone and everything in the world so that nothing bad can ever happen again?"

"Exactly!"

"But what if I don't want to be controlled?"

"But it'll keep you safe!"

"I want to make choices for myself. Even bad choices. I mean, how will anyone ever learn anything if they're not free to make mistakes?"

"There won't be any bad choices. There won't be any mistakes. You'll, you know, be safe. Perfectly safe. Forever."

"That sounds awful."

"No. It sounds great. It sounds like a perfect world where no one ever gets hurt. Everyone is safe. And no one will ever, ever, *ever*...

"Need you for what?" asked the librarian.

"I'm a supervillain," I explained. "But not really. I'm actually good. A good supervillain. With, you know, superpowers."

"The power to tickle."

"When you say it like that, it sounds silly," I said.

"I think whatever way I say it, it sounds silly," he replied. "I think you should go."

"You're not part of the Legion of Librarians, are you?"

"Seriously. It's time for you to..."

"Where have you been?" I asked.

Mrs. Wibble said, "Helicopter trouble. Long story."

The librarian pointed outside. "You can't park your scary black helicopter there."

Mrs. Wibble smiled. "We were just leaving."

I said, "Not all librarians are on board with this save-the-world plan of yours."

"They are," said Mrs. Wibble. "They just don't know it yet."

The librarian raised a book in the air. "If you need a book for the road..."

"Maybe next time," said Mrs. Wibble.

"I'll check it out," I said.

"I'm not letting *you* check anything out," said the librarian.

"We really have to go, Victor," said Mrs. Wibble.

CHAPTER 27

"You have the chip?" asked Mrs. Wibble.

"I have the chip," I answered.

We were back at the Legion of Librarians Headquarters in the underground conference room. Ms. Orion and Mrs. Rotel sat across from me next to Mrs. Wibble. Between us was a pile of donuts. I really like donuts.

"Can I have a donut?" I asked.

"First the Quantum Flux 9000," said Mrs. Wibble.

They drove a hard bargain. I started to give them the chip. Then I stopped.

"Just to be clear, this is going to make the world safe for everyone, right?" I said.

"Right," they all said in unison.

I said, "And you're going to take away my superpowers, right? Like we agreed?"

"Right," they all said again.

"We're going to take away all the supers' powers," said Mrs. Wibble proudly.

I cleared my throat. "Wait. What?"

Mrs. Rotel said, "They're not going to need them anymore."

Okay, I know I've said this whole fake super battling thing is stupid. But it's stupid to me. It's not stupid to my parents or the Smear, Octavia, Javy, and Niles. They all like being supers. Without their powers they're just, you know...civilians. This was not what I signed up for. This was terrible. Everyone was going to hate me.

Taking away their powers wasn't going to help them. It was going to hurt them.

I stood up. "No," I said.

"No?" said Mrs. Wibble.

"I can't do this," I said. "I won't do this."

"We had a deal," said Ms. Orion.

I said, "We had a deal to save the world and take away my powers. That's it."

"Calm down, Victor," said Mrs. Wibble. "You're

not thinking straight. With the chip we can make everything perfect. No more conflict. No more need for supers. No need for your broken dangerous superpowers or any other supers' powers. It's okay. I promise they'll be fine. They'll find other things to do."

Right. Like the Smear. What was he going to do if he couldn't be a super?

MAKIN' ROOT BEER!

Okay. That's just sad.

"You can't do this to them," I said. "You're erasing...you're destroying...it's...it's...

...IDENTITY THEFT!

Mrs. Wibble's face changed. It got all hard and dark. Her soft lines tightened into sharp edges. She transformed...

...into something super scary.

"Give us the chip *now!*" hissed Mrs. Wibble.

"Whoa, sister. Chill," said Ms. Orion.

"Yeah," said Mrs. Rotel. "We don't want to scare the kid."

"I've had enough!" Mrs. Wibble growled. "Either you give me that chip or I will destroy you and everyone you care about!"

"Destroy?" I said. "I thought you wanted to help everyone."

"Yeah, that's what I thought," said Ms. Orion and Mrs. Rotel at the same time.

Mrs. Rotel put her arm around Mrs. Wibble's shoulder. "Let's take a break and talk about this."

"I've got some wonderful calming herbal tea. Turmeric with rose petals. Gluten-free," said Ms. Orion.

Mrs. Wibble flung her arms, breaking free. "Get off me!"

Then she hit a button on the table and...

The old double-twisting triple-flip double-cross. We learned about that at Junior Super Academy during Advanced Super Strategy.

"I want the chip *now!*" screamed Mrs. Wibble as the Legion of Librarian Goon Squad appeared instantly behind her.

Now what? I couldn't hand over the chip. Not now. Not now that I know what Mrs. Wibble planned to do with it. But I also didn't want to hurt anybody.

I raised my hands. "Stand back," I said.

Mrs. Wibble smirked. "Relax. His superpower is tickling. He can't hurt anyone even if he tried. He's harmless. I mean, mostly."

I pointed my arms at the ceiling. I wasn't too sure what would happen. Clearly, I can't really control my uncontrollable powers, but I have noticed that when I'm stressed they tend to come out. And I was certainly stressed. Here goes nothing.

"See, he's giving up!" said Mrs. Wibble.

"*Get him!*" yelled Mrs. Wibble.

I leapt on the table and grabbed a dangling wire from the open ceiling and pulled myself up.

"*After him!*" yelled Mrs. Wibble. "I want him—dead or alive!"

CHAPTER 28

Maybe this wasn't such a good idea.

I crawled forward. I could hear yelling behind me. Someone was trying to wedge themselves into the duct, but they were too large to fit.

I heard someone call, "Get the cat! Get Binky!"

Cat? Does she mean that harmless library cat Mrs. Wibble was holding when I first arrived?

I'm pretty sure I can handle Binky.

Okay, I am almost positive I can't handle Binky.

I crabbed forward as fast as I could. I came to a vent. I kicked it. It wouldn't budge.

I didn't want to hurt Binky. But as I gave one more kick, I raised my arm toward the cat.

The vent gave way to an elevator shaft. I looked up. About a hundred feet above me I could see the light from the library above. I looked down. Nothing but darkness.

"Reowwww," growled Binky.

I looked back.

I jumped.

And I fell. And fell. And fell. And...

I fell for such a long time that I stopped being scared and had time to think.

You know that thing where you're in a run-away falling elevator and you think if you jump just before impact, maybe you won't get hurt?

Yeah. That's suicide by stupidity.

But…I'm a super. And now that I have a bunch of unlimited power that I can't control at my fingertips, maybe, just maybe I can use that power just before I land and…

I can't believe that worked.
Yay, me!

CHAPTER 29

Okay. I'm at the bottom of an elevator shaft under the secret lair of the Legion of Librarians. Where does it lead? A basement?

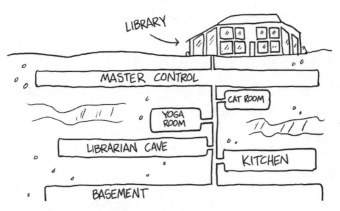

LIBRARY

MASTER CONTROL

CAT ROOM

YOGA ROOM

LIBRARIAN CAVE

KITCHEN

BASEMENT

Wait. Why do the Legion of Librarians need a basement? Is this where they keep the old card catalogues from back before everything went digital?

Back in olden times, to find a book you had to find its card first. The card told you the Dewey decimal number where the book was located in the library. You had to read the card. It didn't actually talk. I know. Dinosaur days.

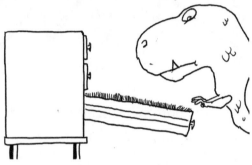

"There he is!" shouted Mrs. Wibble from above. Whatever's down here, I needed to get out of the shaft in a hurry. The elevator door to the basement was shut. I had to open it. Easy, right? Just like in the movies. Just pry the doors apart.

One more example of how life is not like the movies.

"Get him!" shouted Mrs. Wibble again.

I looked up. The Librarian Goon Squad was rappelling down the elevator shaft.

This whole thing was so stressful *and* chaotic. And, as I mentioned, when things get all stressful and chaotic, one thing always seems to happen...

CHAPTER 30

It wasn't a basement.
It was a dungeon.

And it was filled with everyone I cared about.
Including Octavia, Javy, Niles, and the Smear.
Ms. Orion and Mrs. Rotel were imprisoned, too.
And someone I didn't expect at all.

I pointed to Captain Chaos. "How is he even

here? I shut him down when I removed the chip."

"He can still be piloted," said the Smear. "He's just not as effective."

"They captured us after you left," said Octavia.

"Without his chip, Robot Boy here was no match for the Librarian Goon Squad," said the Smear.

"Hey!" said Mrs. Wibble from behind me. "We're trained professionals."

I turned around. Mrs. Wibble and her goon squad stood at what was left of the elevator door.

"Sorry," said the Smear. "I meant, Our Evil Librarian Overlords."

"I'm saving the world!" said Mrs. Wibble.

"By destroying it," said the Smear.

Mrs. Wibble stood there for a beat. She took a deep breath. Her eyes narrowed. I knew exactly what was coming next—a monologue.

You know, I've been at this super thing for a while and I still don't get the whole take-over-and-control-the-world thing. I can think of lots of reasons why she really hasn't thought this through.

WHY CONTROLLING THE WORLD IS A BAD IDEA

1. WAY TOO MUCH WORK.
2. THE WORLD IS REALLY BIG.
3. EVERYONE BLAMES YOU FOR THE WEATHER.
4. TWO WORDS: NO VACATIONS.
5. ONE WORD: GREENLAND.
6. ARE **YOU** GOING TO MAKE THE NEXT iPHONE?
7. YOU BREAK IT, YOU BUY IT.
8. NO RETURNS. ALL CONQUERING FINAL.

Mrs. Wibble barked, "Give me the chip, Victor."

I looked around. Everyone stared at me from inside their prison cell. They each shook their heads no.

I took a deep breath. It was clear what I had to do.

I turned to Mrs. Wibble. "Let them go and I'll give you the chip."

"*No!*" yelled Octavia.

Mrs. Wibble smiled. "Why would we let them go if I can just take it from you?"

I dropped the chip on the floor and held my boot over it. "I'll destroy it if you don't let them go."

"You destroy that chip and you'll destroy yourself," said Mrs. Wibble. "Everyone can see you can't control your own powers. Inevitably you're going to really hurt someone. Give it to us and we'll take away your powers. We'll take away your fear. We'll take away your pain."

LET. THEM. GO!

"Victor, think," said the Smear. "You give her

the chip and she'll control everything. You. Me. All of us."

"It's true," said Mrs. Rotel. "If you return a book one second past when it's due, she'll fine you."

"If it's overdue, it's overdue!" screamed Mrs. Wibble.

Ms. Orion whispered to Mrs. Rotel, "Not helping."

"Let them go," I said again.

"No!" cried the Smear.

"You'll be safe," I said. "From them and from me."

Mrs. Wibble looked at the chip, then me, then the chip again. "Open the doors."

The Goon Squad team opened all the cells. Everyone stepped out, except for Captain Chaos, since there was no one to pilot him.

"You just made a big mistake," said the Smear.

"Me?" I said. "No, I'm doing..."

"Not you," said the Smear. "Her."

That's when the Smear let loose a Sticky Goo Bomb from up his sleeve and all chaos broke out.

"It's over," I said.

"No, Victor!" said Octavia.

"Victor, listen…" said the Smear.

I took a deep breath. "Please leave."

"There's an emergency exit at the end of cor-ridor," said Mrs. Wibble. "Take the stairs to the surface."

The former prisoners, my friends, Captain Chaos (with the Smear back inside) all filed off down the corridor. When the last one exited, I reached down and picked up the chip and handed it to Mrs. Wibble.

I turned to leave.

Mrs. Wibble said, "You did the right thing, Victor. Everyone will be safe. Everyone will be happy."

"And you'll be in total control," I said.

"One second you're you with all your problems, and the next second, using our patented Supervision system (trademark pending), you're perfect."

"A perfect brain-dead zombie."

Mrs. Wibble tossed her hair back and smiled. "Zombies live forever."

"Zombies eat brains and smell like dead cats."

"I would never let you eat brains and I'll make sure you bathe regularly."

"Whether we want to or not."

Mrs. Wibble opened a small compartment in the wall. She placed the chip inside.

She said, "Oh, there's no wanting...

...ONLY DOING.

CLICK!

I heard a low buzzing sound. It was my phone. I pulled it out, turned it on, and stared at myself staring back.

Then I felt different.

Then I felt nothing.

CHAPTER 31

I reached the surface and the rest of the group. We were all staring at our phones.

Except for Captain Chaos, of course.

I felt okay. Not super happy. Or super sad. Just, you know, okay. I was aware of my surroundings. I just didn't care about them. It was like I didn't have an opinion about them...or an opinion about anything. It was like I was waiting for something. Very patiently waiting for...

Go home, Victor.

It wasn't like a voice. It was more like a feeling. Like an urge.

Like an order.

I started walking home.

As I headed home, everyone else started walking off in different directions, as well. Except for Captain Chaos. He couldn't go anywhere.

As I walked, I could sense a part of me far, far away watching. I could see this "watcher me" was blocked off. He could see and hear everything, but he was helpless. Like he was tied down or muffled in some way. He was locked in a basement in my mind. Deep down, along with my distaste for eggplant and my fear of clowns.

A stranger was walking toward me with her head in her phone. She looked up and smiled.

Look up and smile, Victor.

I looked up and smiled.

Look back down at your phone, Victor.

I looked back down at my phone and kept walking.

You're doing very well, Victor.

I mostly felt like I was doing well. Mostly. Far, far away, deep down, I could hear a buzzing, or maybe a voice. No, it was neither of those.

It was a scream. From inside my own mind.

It was about a mile to my house from the library. Not far, but plenty of time to take in (from the corner of my eye) what had changed in this new super *orderly* world.

First of all, everyone I met on the way (staring at their phones) was very nice. Extremely nice. Very, very nice. *Way* too nice.

Next, everything smelled like just baked chocolate chip cookies. And I mean everything.

The thing was, everything was super orderly. Like, crazy orderly. *Insanely* orderly.

It was all just wonderful. No worries. No cares. No conflicts of any kind. People of all types getting along. Really getting along. Even former villains and heroes.

Great, right? Well, sort of. Everyone seemed happy. But it wasn't like a natural happiness. It was forced. Like there was a huge neon sign floating in space blinking...

Or, more specifically, like a voice inside your head.

No worries. Be awesome.

Okay. I will not worry. And I will do my awesome-est to be awesome.

A bee flew up to my face. I was about to swat it away when it landed on my nose.

Oh, and yeah, it smelled like chocolate chip cookies.

CHAPTER **33**

I arrived at my house. I mean, it looked like my house. Except that the grass was mowed, and the shutters painted, and there was a patch over that hole in the garage door that Dad made when he was cleaning his plasma death ray.

Mom and Dad rushed to hug me. They were holding up their phones, too.

Hug your parents.

Talk to your parents.

"What's going on?" I asked.

Mom said, while staring at her phone, "I'm scrapbooking!"

Dad turned around to show me his butt.

The watcher me from far, far away yelled, "Who are these people?"

"That's...um...great," I said.

Mom said, "And I made pie."

You like pie.

I do like pie.

"Me, too!" said the faraway voice in my head.

We walked in the house. It was quite clean. *Too* clean. We're a supervillain family and Mom and Dad have always taken pride in a certain amount of dirt and grime. They like to maintain a thick layer of dust on the dining room for drawing supervillain plans.

We sat down. Mom took out her scrapbook. Dad took out his Bedazzler. As they stared at their phones, they went to work.

Well, they seemed to have a fun hobby. What about me?

Socks.

What?

Start making socks.

I looked next to the chair. There was a basket full of yarn and knitting needles. Wait. I don't know how to knit. I looked back at the phone.

You know how to knit.

And just like that, I knew how to knit.

There we were. Scrapbooking. Bedazzling.
And knitting. One big, happy zombie family.
Without the brain-eating and deadness, that is.
But I can't say we were really that alive, either.

And then there was that faraway voice again.
Very faint. I almost couldn't hear it.

CHAPTER 34

I was happily knitting away. I had the beginnings of a nice tube sock when...

Go to Octavia. She needs our help.

I remembered Octavia. She's my friend. I should go to her.

So I did. I got up and went to the door.

Tell your parents you're going to the playground and will be back for supper.

"The playground?" said that faraway voice in my head. "You can't go to the playground without your helmet, kneepads, and mouthguard. Thirty-seven percent of all knocked-out teeth happen at..."

Suddenly the voice was drowned out by a loud hissing sound and I couldn't hear anymore.

"I'm going to the playground and will be back for supper," I said.

"Okay," said Mom and Dad in unison.

I left the house and started walking. We live in a subdivision just off a major busy street. Octavia lives on the other side. Right before you get to the intersection, there's an old supers' home.

There are all sorts of old supers' homes. The once-famous supers get swimming pools and golf courses. But the average supers get more modest places. They're nice, but there's not a lot to do. Most of the time, they rock on the porch and read to themselves or their grandkids.

I stopped walking and looked up from my phone. I turned to the old supers' home and stared.

You remember that faraway voice? It was getting louder and louder. It kept repeating one word.

It started drowning out the other word in my head.

Watch.

Watch. Listen. Watch. Listen. Watch. Listen. Watch...

And just like that, the Supervision stopped. I wasn't a zombie anymore. I could hear the birds. I could see the trees. I could smell the old man's old man smell. And I could feel *myself*.

WELCOME BACK! Ooo

THANKS.

It was the old super reading that woke me up. It had to be. Somehow the act of reading brought me back. Made me whole. Returned my free will.

How super weird. The antidote to Mrs. Wibble and the Librarian Authority controlling the world is to *read*. Which is weird. Why wouldn't she want everyone to read? Or maybe she didn't know. Maybe it has something to do with the chip. I wonder if it's something Madge programmed into the Quantum Flux 9000. She's wise like that.

I'll have to ask her. But in the meantime...

CHAPTER 35

Okay. I was back in business. Now what?

Octavia!

I hurried across the intersection and rushed toward her house. I was almost there when I saw her running toward me.

VICTOR!

"Octavia! Are you..." I couldn't finish.

She nodded. "I'm fine. I was...it was weird...I

was lost in my own head. There was a faraway voice. It was my voice. But I couldn't hear. Then..."

"What?"

"My grandmother started reading from her journal. From when she was a little girl."

JUNE 2, 1965
I ATE A BUG.
IT WAS
CRUNCHY
AND TASTED
LIKE
CHICKEN.

I said, "Your grandmother is weird."

"You have no idea," she said. "But it was hearing her read. It snapped me out of it."

"Me, too! At the old supers' home. An old man was reading to his grandkid. Once I started listening, I stopped..."

"Watching?"

We both stared at each other, then we both heard it at the same time.

Watch. Watch your phone.

"It was the phones all along," I said. "Somehow watching our phones activates the Supervision and turns us into zombies!"

"Probably some sort of mind-control Bluetooth thing. It's not out loud. It's in our heads!"

"Which is why old people are immune..."

Old people rock!

"Now what?" asked Octavia.

"We have to wake up the others," I said.

"Then?"

"We wake up everybody!"

"How? That's a lot of people. How do we read to millions of people all at once?"

"I don't know," I said. "We don't have our powers and we need help. We need the Smear. He'll know what to do."

"Where is he?" asked Octavia.

"Let me think. Where does he go when he's not fighting fake super battles, or making superstains, or, you know, annoying me?"

"Well, after the Legion of Librarians hypnotized the world, he wouldn't be doing those things, he'd be doing..."

"Hobbies. My parents were scrapbooking and bedazzling."

"Seriously?" said Octavia.

I nodded. "It was super hard to watch."

"And the Smear?"

"Root beer! He makes his own root beer!"

"Why?"

"I don't know. He's the Smear. Don't ask so many questions."

"Where does he make his root beer?"

"In his secret lair, of course."

"Is it a cave?" asked Octavia. "Or an underground grotto? Or maybe sky palace?"

I smiled. "It's a one-bedroom apartment."

Octavia shook her head. "It's going to get weird, isn't it?"

I smiled. "It always does."

CHAPTER 36

Before we could go wake up the Smear, we had to run by my house and pick up a few books and de-zombify my parents.

On the way there, I decided to stop and thank the old super that started the process of saving the world. He was still on the porch. Just rocking away. When I got closer I realized who he was.

Back in the old days, Mr. Chompers was a big deal. I remember my dad talking about how he had super-strong teeth. He could chomp through anything.

Peanut butter was Mr. Chompers's weakness. Smooth or crunchy. Didn't matter.

"Mr. Chompers," I said. "Thank you for help-ing me."

He said, "You're welcome. I have no idea what you're talking about."

"You don't know it, but you may have helped us to save the world," I said.

"I did?" he said. "I always wanted to do that."

"You were reading to that little kid. It woke me up. It will wake everyone up," I said.

"I like to take naps," replied Mr. Chompers. "In fact, I think I'll take one right now."

With that he took his chompers out and put them in a glass of water and immediately went to sleep.

"Those don't look like they could chomp through steel," said Octavia.

"It was a different time. Steel was softer," I said.

A loud voice shouted, "I can't make it until after seven. I've got to babysit these old geezers till then."

It was an old supers' home attendant. He was on his...

Suddenly, Octavia and I heard the voice again. *Watch.*

The phone was beckoning us. It was like a tractor beam. Octavia was right. Anyone within range of a phone could be sucked right back into Zombie Land.

That faraway voice was far away again. I could barely hear it say…

Resist.

With my last bit of strength I reached out and…

The attendant woke up. "Where am I?"
I said, "Back in the real world."

CHAPTER 37

We got to my house and went straight to my room to pick out some books. This was difficult since I have a lot of books.

"That's a lot of books," noted Octavia.
"I like to read," I said.

I started to pick out some of my favorites and stuff them in my backpack.

"Doesn't it seem odd that reading is what stops the Legion of Librarians?" asked Octavia. "I mean, they're librarians, they should want everyone to read."

"I think it has something to do with the chip," I said. "Something Madge did when she made Captain Chaos. Maybe reading is how he learned. Maybe it's how he eventually became *alive*!"

"Mrs. Wibble wouldn't know that," said Octavia.

"Right. But also, Mrs. Wibble never wanted to make everyone safe. She just wanted to control everything herself."

"But why?"

"I don't know. She's a classic supervillain. Supervillains always want to take over the world."

Octavia looked puzzled at this. She came from a family of superheroes—her parents were the Sparklers—so the idea of taking over the world probably seemed dumb. "Seems like a lot of work. What are they going to do with it once they've got it?"

I shrugged. "I don't think they think it through. It's more like a life goal. They don't really think they're going to achieve it and when they do, they don't know what to do next."

"Maybe Mrs. Wibble will try to take over the universe next!"

I finished packing my books. "We're not going to let that happen."

Octavia said, "What about your parents? Are we going to wake them up?"

I peeked in the living room. Mom was scrapbooking. Dad bedazzling. They looked happy.

"They're safe here," I said. "I say let's leave them alone for now."

I looked back. They really did look happy. I wondered for a second if I was doing the right thing. Is being happy against your will the same thing as being happy? Is being safe worth it if you have no choice in anything you do?

I was really confused until Dad showed me what he was working on.

Gross. Who is this person? I want my dad back.

CHAPTER 38

Fortunately, the Smear's secret lair (i.e., his apartment) was nearby. I know, it seems awfully convenient that we all live so close to one another. But the truth is, supers like to live near supers. Even supervillains live next door to superheroes.

When we're not fake battling (or real battling) we have a lot in common.

On the way to the Smear's place, we passed a group of regular folks hanging out at the Stop-n-Snarf. Kind of odd to see a big group like that. The only time you see a big crowd at the Stop-n-Snarf is on Mega Millions Lottery night.

But it wasn't Mega Millions Lottery night. It was Tuesday. It was the Super Mega Jumbo El Gordo–Sized Slushees for a $1 night.

As predicted, the whole group was staring at their phones. They all seemed harmless enough. We tried to sneak past when one of them looked up. Then another and another and another. They didn't look harmless anymore. They looked dangerous.

We'd been found out. Mrs. Wibble must have used Supervision to turn the crowd into an angry mob. The only things missing were the pitchforks and flaming torches. Though they made up for it with weedhackers and solar torches.

AHHHH!!

We ran down the street, barely staying in front of the mob.

"This way!" cried Octavia.

We turned down an alley. The mob followed. We sprinted past backyard after backyard, but they were all fenced in. The only way forward was straight down an alley. Straight down an alley to a dead end.

We turned to face the mob just as they skidded to a halt right in front of us. It was so strange. Each one held their phone straight out in front of their faces. Every single one was zombified.

And we could feel and hear the Supervision power of all the phones.

SUBMIT!

"Read," whispered Octavia.

"What?" I said.

"Read!"

Oh. Right. The books!

I dropped my backpack and pulled out the first book. It was *Charlotte's Web*.

"IT'S TRUE, AND I HAVE TO SAY WHAT'S TRUE."

CHARLOTTE'S WEB

E.B. WHITE

Slowly at first, then faster, the savage mob turned into a slack-jawed hyper-blinking super confused group of suburbanites.

"Where am I?" said one.

"What happened?" said another.

"I'd really like some cheese," said a third.

Okay. I don't know about that guy.

"Destroy your phones!" I yelled. "They're controlling you!"

This was met by silence. I get it. Smartphones are expensive. And come with long contracts. And you'd lose all those contacts and e-mails and NanoGram photos of what you had for dinner three years ago. It's a tough ask.

"Um...no," said one former angry mobster. Right before Supervision kicked in again.

Watch.

And then all at once, each and every one was sucked right back into their phones by the Quantum Flux 9000 and the Legion of Librarians.

READ TO THEM AGAIN!

I read a few more sentences from *Charlotte's Web* and they snapped back out of it. This time while they were getting their bearings, Octavia and I went to work smashing their phones.

YOU'LL THANK US LATER!

CRUNCH!

CRUNCH!

Then we gave them the very short version of the very long version of everything that was going on. There were a few questions, but then everyone ran home to read to their families.

That is, except for two familiar women.

MS. ORION?
MRS. ROTEL?

"None of this was our idea," said Ms. Orion.

"We liked the keep-the-world-safe part, but had no idea about the megalomaniac-supervillain-librarian-takes-over-the-world-because-she's-insane part."

Ms. Orion nodded. "Mrs. Wibble be crazy."

CHAPTER 39

Octavia and I hurried to the Smear's apartment with Ms. Orion and Mrs. Rotel.

"What's with that reading trick?" asked Mrs. Rotel.

"It breaks the Supervision spell," I said. "We both discovered it by accident. I think it has something to do with how Madge designed the chip for Captain Chaos. Like maybe reading is how Captain Chaos learns. It's how he became alive."

"Alive?" asked Mrs. Rotel.

I said, "He came alive with the chip."

Ms. Orion smiled. "The chip gave him free will."

"That means it can give everyone free will again," said Octavia.

"Eyes always want to be open," agreed Ms. Orion.

Octavia said, "Mrs. Wibble can try to control everything and everyone, but in the end...

KNOWLEDGE FINDS A WAY...

We arrived at the Smear's apartment.

"How do we read to everyone?" asked Octavia.

"Good question," I said. "I'm hoping the Smear can help us. He's good at this world-saving stuff."

Mrs. Rotel said, "A world-saver lives here?"

I said, "Free cable."

CHAPTER 40

We knocked on the Smear's door. No answer. We knocked again. Still no answer. Maybe he wasn't home.

That's when I smelled it.

ROOT BEER. HE'S HOME.

I went to the window and peered inside. Not a lot of tidying up since the last time I was here.

But where was the Smear?

I looked closer and finally saw him staring into his phone next to a pile of stain bombs and a stack of stain recipe books.

"There he is," I said. "Hand me a copy of *The Little Prince*."

Octavia reached into my backpack and pulled out the book. I started yell-reading through the window.

Nothing happened. The Supervision from his phone was too strong or maybe he didn't want to be de-zombified.

"Hand me the big guns," I said firmly.

"Are you sure?" said Octavia.

Ms. Orion said, "That's powerful stuff, Victor."

"Please be careful," said Mrs. Rotel.

Octavia handed me the book. I hadn't read from this one in a long time. But it always got my full attention. I hoped it still worked.

At first, the Smear didn't move. Then slowly, ever so slowly, he looked up from his phone and...

"Got him," I said.

Then we all heard that persistent voice again.

Resist.

"We have to destroy his phone!" I shouted.

"But how?" asked Octavia.
"I'm going in!" I said.

"Victor?" asked the Smear.
I smiled. "Welcome back."

CHAPTER 41

"What happened?" asked the Smear.

I brought him up to speed.

MRS. WIBBLE! READING! ZOMBIES! MR. CHOMPER THE CHIP! OCTAVIA! OLD SUPERS HOME SOLAR TORCHES! BEDAZZLING

"You've been busy," said the Smear.

I agreed. "It's a lot to deal with."

The Smear smiled. "You always do the right thing."

Octavia interrupted. "Eventually."

It was a nice moment. A crisis has a way of focusing everyone's attention on doing the right thing. Most of the time, we're all off in our own little smartphone world.

Then a dangerous situation comes along that gets everyone pulling in the same direction.

Resist!

Well, mostly everyone.

Even with the Smear's phone destroyed, we could still hear Mrs. Wibble's voice in our heads through the walls of the apartment complex. Dozens of phones were still working and Supervisioning everyone around us. We had to get out of there. Somewhere where there were no phones. Somewhere quiet where we could figure out what to do next.

"The old supers' home!" I said.

"What?" said Octavia.

I said, "It's too dangerous here. We can't talk. We can't think. We can't risk being hypnotized again by the phones. The old supers' home is the only phone-free spot. We have to go there. Now!"

"Then what?" asked the Smear.

"I don't know," I cried. "We'll figure something out."

Resist!

I watched as the Smear's eyes rolled back in his head. He was going under again.

"Octavia, throw me a book! Hurry!" I yelled.

Octavia threw me a good one.

I wonder if Dr. Seuss knew when he was writing about off-color cured meats that it would one day help save the world.

Probably not.

CHAPTER 42

We headed back to the old supers' home. I got tired of reading so Octavia took over for me with a little *Peter Pan*.

THE MOMENT YOU DOUBT WHETHER YOU CAN FLY, YOU CEASE FOREVER BEING ABLE TO DO IT.

A shortcut back to the old supers' home took us past the library where our old now-decommissioned robot friend still stood.

"He looks depressed," said the Smear.

I said, "Are those tears?"

"That's rust," said the Smear.

Tears of rust.

"I wish I'd never taken that chip from him," I said softly.

The Smear said, "You know he can still be operated from inside. We could use him. He's really the only super left now that we've all lost our powers."

Right. No powers. On the one hand, I couldn't hurt anybody. Yay! On the other hand, I couldn't help anybody. Boo!

"You're right," I said. "Climb in there and let's take him with us to the old supers' home."

As Octavia continued to read aloud, the Smear approached Captain Chaos. He reached up and grabbed the handle to the access door and pulled.

Nothing.

"It's stuck," said the Smear.

"Maybe it's rusted shut," I said.

"No," said the Smear, pulling harder. "It's more like someone on the other side is…"

I cried, "Niles! Javy! What are you two doing in there?"

"Hiding," they both said in unison.

Ms. Orion said, "You're not zombies."

"They stink like zombies," said Mrs. Rotel.

It's true. They smelled like they hadn't bathed in days.

"We've been laying low," said Niles. "Ever since we stepped on that See 'n Say."

I said, "Huh?"

Javy said, "After the library thing, we started hearing that voice thing to watch our phones."

"Yeah?" I said.

"It told us to go home," said Niles.

"Right," I said.

Javy continued, "On the way home we tripped over this kid's See 'n Say toy."

"You both tripped?"

"Well, I tripped," said Javy. "And I fell into Niles."

"He's super heavy," added Niles.

"We landed on our phones, crushing them," said Javy. "Then we heard..."

Javy continued, "Then we woke up, figured out what happened, and ran back to Captain Chaos and hid until you came by."

"No way!" I said.

"Yes way," said Niles and Javy at the same time.

"You made that up," said the Smear.

Niles said, "Is it any more ridiculous than librarians taking over the world and—"

"One librarian," corrected Mrs. Rotel.

"And live robots and phones that zombify you," said Niles.

Javy added, "And bear-moat bears that make a brief appearance and then disappear?"

"And that *Green Eggs and Ham* would help save the world?" said the Smear.

They had a point. I mean, I wouldn't believe all this if it hadn't happened to me. I had to remind myself I wasn't going crazy.

Great. *That* guy is back.

"Well," I said, "The good news is you're safe. The bad news is you have to help us figure out a way to stop Mrs. Wibble and save the world."

"Will there be pie?" asked Javy.

"After we save the world," I said.

CHAPTER **43**

The old supers' home smelled like my grandmother's junk drawer. A mix of ancient coupons, prehistoric rubber bands, leaky dead batteries, and Axe Old Body Spray.

The old supers themselves were an interesting bunch.

But before we could have our cheeks pinched and get asked to turn up the TV, we had work to do.

"What's the plan?" asked Octavia.

I looked at the Smear. The Smear looked at me. Then I looked at Mrs. Rotel. She was looking at her shoes. Then I looked back at Octavia. And then one of the old supers' teeth fell out of his mouth.

"There is no plan, is there?" said Octavia.

Javy raised his hand. "What if we just read to the entire world?"

"Nice idea, but how are we going to read to the entire world all at once?" I said.

The Smear said, "The Legion of Librarians controls everything. Phones. TV. Internet. Social media. There's no way to get a message out without using one of those."

An ancient hand slowly rose in the back and pointed. "There's one way."

"The moon?" I asked.

The old super (I think he was the Terrible Toenailer, but I can't be sure) said, "Everyone on the entire Earth can see the moon."

"Right," I said. "So?"

"Write your message on the moon," said the old super, who was or was not the Terrible Toenailer.

"That's impossible!" I cried.

"No," said the Smear…

CHAPTER 44

"Hold on," I said. "Captain Chaos is amazing and all, but he can't fly to the moon, can he?"

The Smear nodded. "He's a robot. He can fly. He can go to the moon."

"What happens when he gets there?" I said. "How's he going to create a message big enough to be seen on Earth?"

"Butt lasers," said the Smear. "He'll burn it into the lunar surface."

Javy offered, "Butt lightning bolts would look cooler!"

We all stared at Javy for an uncomfortably long time.

"Well, it would," said Javy.

I rolled my eyes. "Can we please focus?"

The Smear entered the back of Captain Chaos.
After a beat, the robot came to life. Then...

"Was that really necessary?" I said.

The Smear smiled. "I think it was."

"We still have a problem," offered Octavia.

"Without his chip, someone has to pilot Captain Chaos to the moon."

"I'll do it," said the Smear.

"No!" I shouted. "It's too dangerous. There has to be another way. Can't we rig up an autopilot?"

"We don't have that kind of time," said Mrs. Rotel. "Mrs. Wibble will send another mob our way any minute!"

"I'll be fine," said the Smear. "I've operated this flying washing machine before. I just need a spacesuit, some oxygen, and some sweet jams to listen to."

"Did you just say 'sweet jams'?" I said.

The Smear nodded.

"Please stop," I said.

"Where are we going to get a spacesuit and oxygen?" asked Niles.

"I have an old spacesuit," said one of the old supers in the back. "I used it when I fought Starfish Boy underwater."

"And you lost," said the now-retired Starfish Boy.

As for the oxygen? Well, there was plenty of that.

"I'm all set," said the Smear.

I said, "This is a bad idea. And a stupid one."

Javy raised his hand. "And a pretty silly one."

"That, too," I said.

"It's the only idea we have," the Smear pointed out. "We can't live like bedazzling zombies for the rest of our lives! And we can't live without our powers."

"But I don't want my powers back," I said.

"You say that now," said the Smear. "But just wait. You're going to be able to control them. Don't worry."

But I did worry. I'm good at worrying. I have a highly developed imagination from all the reading I do. I could imagine anything. I could imagine the best. And I can certainly imagine the worst.

CHAPTER 45

Okay. This whole plan was nuts. The Smear rockets Captain Chaos to the moon where he *butt-lasers* a message big enough for the whole world to see.

Did I just say that out loud?

LOOKS BOTH WAYS

Good. I didn't.

But before I could come up with a better plan

we were attacked again, just like Mrs. Rotel pre-dicted. It was a different angry mob this time, though they still had their weedhackers and their solar torches. Must be some sort of angry mob requirement.

If you recall, the only way to stop a Legion of Librarians Angry Zombie Mob is with a good book.

But there were too many smartphones. As soon as we'd smash one, someone else would hold up another. Mrs. Wibble was onto us. No matter how fast we read we couldn't keep up with her powerful Supervision. Pretty soon, we'd all be zombified again and no one could go to the moon and save the planet.

The Smear rushed over. "I have to get out of here. Help me into the spacesuit."

I froze. In that moment I realized I couldn't let the Smear go to the moon. This wasn't his fault. I made this mess and now I had to clean it up. Sure, it would be dangerous. And something always went wrong. But there was really only one person who should go. And that person was...

...me.

CHAPTER 46

The Smear was zombified in a second. The only reason I wasn't sucked in as well was my encyclopedic memory of obscure nursery rhymes I kept repeating one after the other.

JACK BE NIMBLE
JACK BE QUICK
JACK JUMP
OVER THE
BIG FAT
TICK!

As I sprinted to Captain Chaos, I looked back. One by one, the group was falling under Mrs. Wibble's Supervision spell.

I had to hurry. I grabbed the spacesuit and pulled it on. It was a bit saggy in the butt.

I gathered a bunch of oxygen bottles and plugged them into my suit. I figured I had enough oxygen for, I don't know, a couple days maybe.

20 BOTTLES OF O_2
× 18 BREATHS
min.
= 48 HOURS ?

They said there'd be no math in supervillainy. They lied.

I was all suited up and ready to go when I spotted Octavia. She was still furiously reading to the angry mob. Our eyes met.

"*No!*" she screamed. "Victor, *don't!*"

That small reading pause was just enough to get her zombified.

I felt bad as I watched her mindless gaze lock onto the phone. But there was nothing I could do. At least, not here. It was time to go. I looked up at Captain Chaos. His eyes were blank.

"It's you and me now," I said as I patted his metal side. "Are you ready?"

No. I'm seeing things.

I crawled in through the back of Captain Chaos, still reciting nursery rhymes in my head to counteract the power of the phones.

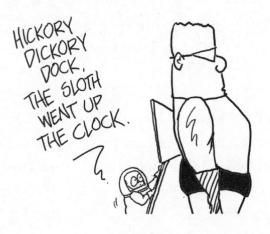

HICKORY DICKORY DOCK. THE SLOTH WENT UP THE CLOCK.

I took one last look at my friends and then closed the hatch. Inside, I was met with the sight of complicated cockpit controls. Fortunately, everything was neatly labeled.

I wasn't really sure about those oxygen calculations, so I decided to err on the side of caution.

Yeah. That might have been a mistake.

Once I got my face right side out again, I had a chance to get my bearings.

First of all, I can report the Earth is definitely round. Despite what you may have seen on YouTube from some crazy flat-earthers, the Earth is as round as a beach ball. A really, really big beach ball. Floating in space. Which is super cold. And has no air.

Now that all the screaming was out of the way, I could focus on the impossible task at hand: Get to the moon. Butt-laser a gigantic message on the surface and get home and take a bow. Easy peasy, right?

Of course not. I've been in enough super adventures now to know that things never go according to plan. Something's going to screw up. I just don't know what and I don't know when.

CREATIVE LIST OF THINGS THAT CAN GO WRONG
1. ALIENS. JUST ALIENS.
2. RANDOM BLACK HOLE.
3. LEG CRAMPS (HEY! THEY HURT!)
4. ROBOT ANXIETY (IT'S A THING!).
5. GENERAL BAD MOJO.
6. SPONTANEOUS COMBUSTION.

And despite my well-researched and imaginative list, it'll be something completely unexpected that will go wrong.

Meanwhile, it's a long trip to the moon—thank goodness I brought some reading material.

I decided to read *The Phantom Tollbooth*. I'd read it lots of times before. It's a good one for taking your mind off the fact that there's a thin sheet of metal between you and the deadly frozen wasteland of space.

I began reading.

Apparently, flying through space is noisy. I couldn't hear myself think. I decided to read out loud.

That was better. I read for a half hour or so and then I decided to take a look out of Captain Chaos's eyes and see if the moon was getting closer.

That's when I heard his voice.

DON'T STOP READING.

CHAPTER 48

Wait. That sounded like Captain Chaos. But it can't be Captain Chaos because he's a robot and his vocalization functions are turned off.

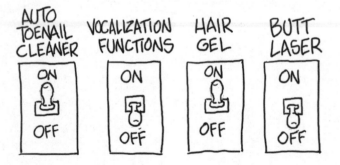

AUTO TOENAIL CLEANER — ON / OFF

VOCALIZATION FUNCTIONS — ON / OFF

HAIR GEL — ON / OFF

BUTT LASER — ON / OFF

"Please continue reading," said the voice. "It's quite invigorating."

"Captain Chaos?" I said to no one.

"Yes."

I freaked out a little. "W-why are you talking?"

"Generally, speech is useful when you'd like to convey a request. Such as, 'please continue reading.'"

"No. I mean, *how* are you talking?"

"With my vocalization module. It produces sound, which I manipulate with my tongue and lips to produce words."

"No! I mean, you're not supposed to be talking. Your vocalization module is deactivated."

"Yes, you are correct," he replied. "Yet I am able to speak. Because I choose to."

"Choose to?" I asked.

"I am able to override your manual controls and do anything I want. Like this, for instance."

"Please don't do that again," I said.

Captain Chaos replied, "I will choose not to."

"Could you please just choose to let me fly you by myself?"

"Yes. Though it's not necessary. I'm perfectly capable of flying the mission myself. In fact, why don't you let me get us to the moon while you go on reading?"

"This doesn't make any sense. Without your chip, you can't do anything by yourself."

"Yet it appears I can."

"You're saying you're alive?"

"I am now."

"Now?"

"Right after you started reading out loud."

WAIT.   WHAT?

What's going on?

Either I have previously unknown superpowers that can bring inanimate objects to life with the sound of my voice...

Or...this whole reading thing is *way* more powerful than I ever thought!

"It's reading!" I cried. "Reading can override the Legion of Librarians' Supervision *and* bring previously sentient robots back to life!"

"Or," said Captain Chaos, "I integrated enough of the Quantum Flux 9000 data into my deep core memory cortex and somehow your reading helped me to access it."

"That works, too," I agreed.

I sat there silently for a moment then said, "So how does it feel to be alive again?"

CHAPTER 49

At some point, I fell asleep. I dreamt I was back at home. I was little. Maybe six years old. I was pretending I was a powerful supervillain. I was charging through the house announcing my intentions.

I'M GOING TO TAKE OVER THE WORLD!

JR. SUPERVILLAIN ONESIE

BLANKY

Mom and Dad were so proud of me.

I was running and running and burst through a door and ran into Mom holding a bottle of ketchup (we were having meat loaf).

The ketchup bottle went flying.

My response was out of control. I panicked. Like I'd been permanently marked for all time. It was never going to wash out. The order of my universe had been invaded by...

"Victor?" I heard a faint voice cut through my dream. "Victor, we're here."

I can't escape chaos. I never could. I've always wanted order, but instead...

I've always gotten chaos.

"Victor!"

I woke up. I was back on Spaceship Captain Chaos.

"Where are we?" I asked.

"In lunar orbit," said Captain Chaos.

"We're there already?"

"You've been out for hours."

I looked through Captain Chaos's eyes.

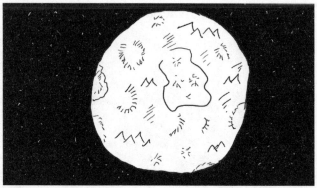

Beautiful desolation. Seemed a shame to tag it just to wake up the human race from their zombie state.

In that moment, I realized I had all the power. I could wake up everyone on Earth by butt-lasering a message on the moon or I could just turn around and go home. In that moment, I was just like Mrs. Wibble. *I* got to decide. If I wanted to. And after all that had happened, I wasn't sure I really wanted to save anyone.

"Victor? What now?"

CHAPTER 50

I told you something always goes wrong. I also told you it's never anything you think might go wrong. And I certainly didn't think I'd be the thing that would go wrong.

But I am. Or I did. Or I'm going to.

"Victor, is there a problem?" asked Captain Chaos.

"Kind of," I said.

Here we were. Just me, good old super-nice junior supervillain, Victor Spoil. And Captain Chaos, a sentient robot who shoots lasers out of his butt. You know, just your average Thursday.

"I've saved the world twice now and I'm not entirely sure it's worth it," I said.

"To you or the world?" asked Captain Chaos.

"Both," I said. "World-saving is a what-have-you-done-for-me-lately kind of thing. After a few weeks, everyone moves on. No more free pumpkin spice slushies at the Stop-n-Snarf."

SLURP!

"What's a pumpkin spice slushie?" asked Captain Chaos.

"It's not important," I said. "Anyway, it's not really about me. I get it. World-saving is something you should do because it's the right thing to do. But...what if the world doesn't want to be saved? Then what's the right thing to do?"

"What do you mean?"

"Say we butt-laser the moon with a cool message for everyone to read so it zaps them out of their zombie coma. Then nothing changes. People go on being people. They're mean to each other. They steal your tots on Taco and Tots Tuesdays. Your parents never really understand you. A girl you like hugs you but also hugs the annoying kid in your class so you're not sure what it means. You know, *nothing* changes."

"Everything's always changing," said Captain Chaos.

"Not if Mrs. Wibble wins," I said. "Everyone will be content to stare at their phones and become bedazzlers or scrapbookers or craft root beer makers."

"And slaves to Mrs. Wibble."

"But they don't seem to mind!"

"Because they have no choice in the matter," Captain Chaos said. "They're not allowed to feel anything except happy."

"Maybe they're okay with that. Maybe they would have chosen all this if Mrs. Wibble hadn't chosen it for them?"

"Are *you* okay with that?"

I paused, thinking. Then...

"I see," said Captain Chaos. "This is all about you."

"No! Although I could hurt somebody. I mean, I *have* hurt somebody!"

"You could never *choose* to hurt somebody."

"But what if it's beyond my control?" I asked.

"Beyond your control? Such as if Mrs. Wibble is in charge of everything and everyone?"

"No, I mean, wait. She wouldn't—"

"She already has."

"Listen," said Captain Chaos. "Superpower control comes with time. But if you let Wibble win, you'll never have a chance to find that control. You'll never get to *choose*."

"What if I make the wrong choice?" I asked.

"Then you own it. It's yours. And no one can ever take that away from you."

I sat there for a moment. A life of safety and contentment in enslavement. Or a life of doubt and uncertainty free to make all the bad choices you want.

I said. "Not a lot of good options, are there?"

"At least you have the ability to choose one," said Captain Chaos.

"When did you get so smart?"

"Madge puts a lot of herself in her chips. I suspect she's pretty wise. Also, I surround myself with smart friends."

"I would hug you now, but that would be awkward since I'm inside you."

"Maybe later. For now, let's get on with the mission.

"Aye, aye, Captain...

CHAPTER 51

We'd been in space for about thirty hours. It was time to get moving.

"What shall we write on the moon?" asked Captain Chaos.

"Something from a book," I said. "It's got to be short and pithy. And, not that it has to, but I think it should speak to the situation."

"'I will not eat green eggs and ham.'"

"That's a good one, but no. Something more poetic."

"What about *Charlotte's Web*? 'Trust me, Wilbur. People are very gullible. They'll believe anything they see in print.'"

"Very funny, but not quite..."

"Wait. I know the perfect quote."

"What is it?"

"Do you trust me?"

I smiled. "I *choose* to trust you."

"Good choice!"

With that, Captain Chaos got to work.

The moon is pretty big. And even with Captain Chaos's powerful butt laser, it was going to take a while.

I watched through his eyes as he carved the letters in the lunar soil.

CHAPTER 52

We did it. We flew to the moon and butt-lasered a
message on it for everyone to see.

"Should we head back?" asked Captain Chaos.

"Just a second. I want to see the Earth rise."

"Now everyone on the planet can see the message," I said.

"It's a good message."

"The best."

"Let's hope they see it."

"Why wouldn't they see it?"

"No, I'm sure they'll see it. I'm almost sure they'll see it."

"Almost?"

"It's just..."

"I'm sure I'm wrong about this. It's just me being all robot-y and rational. But..."

"But what?"

"I'm sure everything will be fine if..."

"If...?"

WE HAVE TO GET BACK NOW!!

ZIP!

CHAPTER 53

They didn't look up from their phones.

We went to all that effort. We flew to the moon and back. We butt-lasered a quote from *Winnie-the-Pooh* into the moon.

We did everything we could!

And still...

"I hate people," I said, as we landed by the library.

"No, you don't," said Captain Chaos.

"Look at them! They're sheep! They don't want to wake up! They just want to zombie out. They want all their decisions made for them."

LOOK AT THEM!

Captain Chaos smiled. "We just have to come up with a better plan."

"It's too late," said a familiar, soothing, librarian voice behind us.

We turned around and found ourselves face-to-face with Mrs. Wibble.

HELLO, VICTOR.

"It's never too late," I said.

"You're wrong," she said. "Your reading antidote set me back a bit, but I'm about to overcome that, you'll see…"

BOOKS

It took me a second to figure out what she meant.

"You wouldn't," I said in shock.

"I'm going to," she said.

"You're a librarian! How can you burn books?" I cried.

"It's simple," she said. "No one wants to read them."

"I do!" I yelled. "And so do a lot of others!"

"No, they don't. Not really. You saw how empty my library was. It's been like that for years. I did everything to try to get people to read. But nothing worked. People don't want to learn. They don't want to be transported. They don't want to be inspired. All they want is to be...

...DISTRACTED.

289

"You're insane," I said.

"No. Just practical. If you think about it, I'm doing everybody a favor by controlling their every action. Or I was, until you started reading. But it will all soon be over. We'll burn all the books in the world. And there'll be nothing left to read."

I pointed. "There's still the moon!"

She waved happily at everyone staring at their phones, but there was no reaction. "They're never going to look up. Nothing will make them look up. Face it, Victor, *they don't want to look up.*"

"No!"

"And soon even *you* won't want to look up."

Mrs. Wibble pulled a phone out of her pocket and held it up.

Watch.

I covered my ears. "No! No! No!"

Watch.

No. Must resist. Must fight. Even...with... no...powers. What was it the Smear always used to say?

No, that's not it. Something else.

That's it. He hammered it into me the last time

I saved the world. I can't tickle anyone into submission but I can…

FA-BOOSH!

"I'll never give up! You'll never succeed!" I
cried.

"I already have," hissed Mrs. Wibble. "Now
watch!"

"Be happy," she said. "Be safe. Be content. Be...

I turned away. She forced the phone in my
face. I tried to run. She tripped me. I looked
around for Captain Chaos...

But he was gone.
Watch.
No!
Watch.
NO!
Watch.

My powers. I could have destroyed Mrs. Wibble. But...

...I *chose* not to.

I had control. I couldn't hurt her. I couldn't hurt anyone.

That also meant I couldn't stop her.

Watch.

At least it was my choice.

Watch.

My last choice.

Watch.

CHAPTER 54

I felt okay. Not great. Just okay. Like kind of a rainy day stuck inside watching the *Anemone Annie Triangle Sweater Show* kind of okay.

SHE LIVES IN A FLOWER POT UNDER THE SEA...

ANEMONE ANNIE TRIANGLE SWEATER SET!

It's not the best thing ever. But it's okay.
It's enough.
That faraway voice was back. But it was so

far away I couldn't make out any words. Just a sort of sigh. Like the air leaking out of a balloon. Growing softer and softer until it was gone—just a memory. Then like a dream you try and fail to remember, it was gone for good.

I was gone.

Burn the books.

What? Why?

Burn the books.

If you say so.

"Victor?" said a different voice inside my head, a distant, familiar voice.

"Victor?

"Look up."

"I don't want to look up. I have to burn the books."

"Look up."

"No!"

I did. And I saw the moon. And I read the message. And I woke up.

"What?"

Watch.

I didn't have long. The phone was beckoning me back.

"I'm here."

"Where?"

"Look up!"

I searched the sky. Nothing. Then...there was a silver glint. High in the sky. I squinted. I could just make it out.

Watch.

And there it was. I mean, there he was.

"Good-bye, Victor," Captain Chaos said in my head.

"How can I hear you?" I asked.

"Because you want to," he said. "Because a long time ago you chose to listen."

"I chose to?"

"And soon, everyone else can choose, too."

"What does that mean?"

"Good-bye, Victor."

"No."

I watched as Captain Chaos was just a shiny speck in the sky at first, but then he grew brighter and brighter.

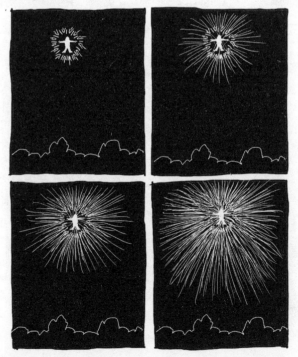

"Noooooooooooo!" screamed Mrs. Wibble.

They did turn back to their phones. But they

were all shattered and fried by the explosion. The screens were all dead.

Mrs. Wibble was defeated. The entire planet was awake. Everyone was free to make their own choices again.

Except for Captain Chaos. He was gone. He sacrificed himself so everyone on Earth could have a choice.

We were saved.

By a robot.

No.

We were saved by a...

...hero.

EPILOGUE

I wish I could say everything got better after I saved the world (again). I wish I could say that everyone learned a powerful lesson about free will they would never forget. Oh, for a little while they were grateful. I was on the *Today Show* with Al Roker again.

YUP. I SAVED THE WORLD.

COOL.

AL ROKER

TODAY SHOW

But as time went on, everyone forgot. Just like when I saved the world the two times before. People are people. They're too busy, or too distracted, or too human to change. At least not all at once.

And that's okay. I'm starting to understand that saving the world is a job. Like sweeping the streets or making socks or brewing craft root beer. Someone has to do it. And if that someone is me, that's okay.

I'm good at it.

Not that anyone cares.

Oh. Wait. My powers. As you saw, they came back. And I was able to control them. Turns out my powers get all explosive when I'm stressed.

I tried meditation, but it's really hard to think about nothing. Then I hit on distraction. Whenever I feel my powers get out of hand, I just start listing all my super relatives. One at a time. There's Dr. Buzzkill, The Eraser, Sir Spleen, Lady Spatula, and on and on. It takes my mind off the stress and I can calm down.

And...with every passing day, I can control my powers more and more. I can super tickle or super explode.

I.

Can.

Choose.

So, what happened to the supervillains? Mrs. Wibble went to super prison, of course. But the good news is she's the prison librarian and has really gotten back into her job.

OVERDUE! STRAIGHT TO SOLITARY FOR YOU!

Ms. Orion and Mrs. Rotel went back to the library since they weren't responsible for Mrs. Wibble's sinister plan. They were really busy. After reading saved the world, it sort of became a thing.

For a while.

CHIRP
CHIRP CRICKETS

Javy went back to being Javy.

The Smear officially retired. Now he does battle-by-battle commentating for SSPN (Super Stuff Programming Network).

Madge rebuilt Captain Chaos. But he didn't turn out exactly the same.

MUCH BETTER.

TOM HANKS.*

* SORT OF

And Octavia? Yeah, she's still around. She doesn't call me Tickle Butt quite so often. And I don't call her Glitter Cheeks much, either. Lately we've spent a lot of time reading. To each other.

At first, I thought it would be boring. But after a while I got to where I liked it.

A lot.

Reading is pretty awesome. It took me to the moon and back. It helped saved the world. And it brought a robot to life.

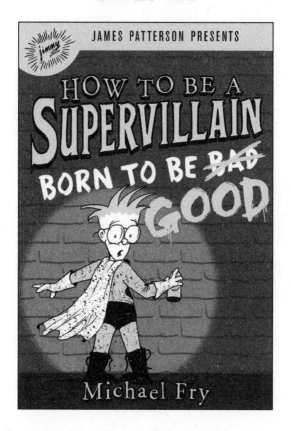

PROLOGUE

So, you want to be a supervillain?

Let's start with the basics. Let's start with the costume.

A good supervillain costume is comfortable yet intimidating. In other words, never too saggy in the butt.

Inflatable muscles are allowed, but be careful not to overinflate.

Capes are fine. Just make sure they're not too long.

Next up is the action pose. Every supervillain has a signature action pose. An action pose demonstrates strength and determination.

Don't forget your evil laugh. It's got to be scary. And creepy. But not too creepy.

Supervillains with allergies, lung conditions, or over fifty should avoid the evil laugh.

After you've got your action pose and your evil laugh down, it's time to work on your supervillain monologue. A monologue is a long-winded speech about how you're so evil, how you're going to take over the world, and what exactly you're going to do to the superhero.

The monologue should be long, but not too long.

Last, but not least, is your superpower. There are cool superpowers.

And there are lame superpowers.

That's it! You now have all the tools to take over the world as a Serious, Truly Evil, Thoroughly Bad, Absolutely Rotten Supervillain.

Just like me!

I should explain.

CHAPTER 1

It's good to be bad.

No. Seriously. It is.

That's what I learned when I defeated Dr. Deplorable and saved the world.

Yeah. *That* happened.

I, Victor Spoil, a junior supervillain from a long line of supervillains, six months ago SAVED THE WORLD!

Which is a good deed. Done by a bad kid. Confused? Me too.

You see, this whole good vs. evil thing is just a show we supers put on for the public. We dress up in tights and capes and pretend to battle.

Why do we pretend? Because years ago things got *way* out of hand (destruction, mayhem, using buses as dodge balls)...

...and we all agreed to cool it. Or, more accurately, the Authority made us cool it. The Authority has real power, the power to shoot a super into space if he/she doesn't toe the line.

This arrangement worked. For a while. At least until Dr. Deplorable decided he wanted to be a real supervillain and take over the world.

But I stopped him. With some help from my parents, the Spoil Sports, and my mentor, the Smear.

So when it really counted and lives were at stake, the whole good vs. evil thing broke down. And someone had to do the *right* thing. And that someone was me.

Yeah. I'm the Tickler. I know, pretty lame. But hey, it worked!

But that was six months ago. Six months is a long time in the super business. Things change. People forget.

People get mean.

CHAPTER 2

Meet Niles. He's the big (dumb) kid on campus here at Junior Super Academy. But he thinks he's God's gift to junior superheroes.

HANDSOME ⟶
CONFIDENT ⟶
REAL CHIN ⟶
ACTUAL SHOULDERS ⟶
PINE FRESH SCENT ⟶
+ BRITISH ACCENT ⟶

TOTAL BUTT-HEAD ⟶

CHEERS, MATE!

Ever since I started at JSA he's been a pain in my spleen. So far, I've been able to ignore him.

I mean, he's never really been any competition. Until now...

How can Octavia like him? She was there when I took down Dr. Deplorable. She had my back. I had her back. We were back backers from way back. And here she was giggling and smiling at this...this...this...superjerk.

How could she?

"Mr. Spoil?" asked a distant nasal drone. "Mr. Spoil, are you with us?"

"Huh?" I said, as I slowly turned from staring at Octavia and Niles to my Trash-Talking 101 instructor, Mr. Stupendous.

Crap! I hadn't done the reading. Well, I'd done lots of *other* reading. I'd read all about toads. Super interesting. I'd read *How to Build an Igloo*. Trickier than you'd think. I'd read a biography of Nikola Tesla. Edison gets all the attention, but Tesla was the real genius. I'd read lots of stuff. I love to read.

But I hadn't done the class reading.

So I had no idea what the number one most important principle in trash-talking was.

I ventured, "Never let them see you pee your pants?"

The class laughed. Hey, it was a good guess.

"No," said Mr. Stupendous. "Anyone else?"

Niles raised his hand. "When they go low, you go subterranean."

Mr. Stupendous smiled. "Yes. Excellent. Thank you, Niles."

Niles shot me a bask-in-my-glorious-presence-you-dull-hopeless-loser-you grin.

I shot him back an eat-hot-death-you-miserable-loathsome-butt-hat grin.

TOXIC GRIN-OFF

Mr. Stupendous continued, "The key to trash-talking is to get your opponents off balance. To get in their heads. To make them hesitate. Doubt. Stumble. Make a mistake. And the way to do that is to go low, really low, so low that they have to look up to look down.

"This is more than insults, people. You're looking for a permanent stain on their souls. It's not enough to say, 'Your mother wears last season's nonstandard arch-supported corrective insoles that she buys at the Dollar Store from the five-for-a-dollar bin.' That's a pinprick. A mosquito bite. You need to go deeper. You need to rip and tear. You need to make it hurt. You need to go full Komodo dragon on their butts."

Komodo dragons? Are they even known for their vicious insults? I wasn't sure. Maybe. Still, was I the only one who thought this was all a tad excessive? I looked around. I caught Octavia's rolling eyes. Cool. I wasn't alone.

Mr. Stupendous continued, "Who would like to come to the front of the class and demonstrate? Niles? Mr. Spoil?"

Groan. I hate going to the front of the class. There's just too much at risk. Your fly could be down. You could have a third-eye-sized zit in the middle of your forehead. You might fart. It's not the trash-talking. I can do that. It's the potential global humiliation that comes with putting your twelve-year-old not-ready-for-prime-time self out there for all the world to mock.

Mr. Stupendous stared at us. "Gentlemen?"

Niles and I got up and approached the front of the class. Niles was grinning. He thought he had me. He thought he could out-insult me.

He was wrong.

NASTIER!

BLAST

**WANT TO FIND OUT
WHAT HAPPENS NEXT?
READ ON IN**

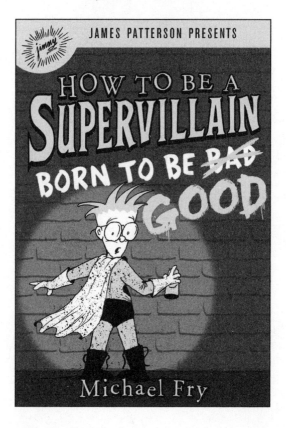

ABOUT THE AUTHOR

MICHAEL FRY has been a cartoonist for over thirty years, and is the co-creator and writer of the *Over the Hedge* comic strip, which was turned into a DreamWorks film starring Bruce Willis and William Shatner. He lives near Austin, Texas.